THE WIDOW'S FIRST KISS

A BILLIONAIRE AND A VIRGIN ROMANCE (DREAMS FULFILLED BOOK 1)

SCARLETT KING

HOT AND STEAMY ROMANCE

CONTENTS

Copyright	v
Sign Up to Receive Free Books	vii
Blurb	ix
1. Chapter 1	1
2. Chapter 2	7
3. Chapter 3	15
4. Chapter 4	25
5. Chapter 5	34
6. Chapter 6	50
7. Chapter 7	58
8. Chapter 8	68
9. Chapter 9	75
10. Chapter 10	85
Sign Up to Receive Free Books	87
Preview of Lucky's Naughty Angel	89
Chapter One	91
Chapter Two	99
Chapter Three	106
Other Books By This Author	115
Copyright	117

COPYRIGHT

Made in "The United States" by:

Scarlett King

© Copyright 2020 –Scarlett King

ISBN: 978-1-64808-026-5

ALL RIGHTS RESERVED. No part of this publication may be reproduced or transmitted in any form whatsoever, electronic, or mechanical, including photocopying, recording, or by any informational storage or retrieval system without express written, dated and signed permission from the author

SIGN UP TO RECEIVE FREE BOOKS

Sign Up to Receive Free E-Books and Audiobook Codes.

Would you like to read **The Unexpected Nanny, Dirty Little Virgin** and **other romance books** for **free**?

You can sign up to receive these free e-books and audiobooks by typing this link into your browser:

https://www.steamyromance.info/free-books-and-audiobooks-hot-and-steamy/

Or this one:

https://www.steamyromance.info/the-unexpected-nanny-free/

BLURB

The afternoon that the mistletoe sprigs appear all over town, impoverished military widow Lorena Webster is about to spend her last twenty dollars so that her daughter Cindy can at least have one Christmas gift. As they walk down to the toy store from the apartment they share with Lorena's sister Andie, they happen to see Lorena's longtime man crush window shopping up ahead.

James Norris is a heartthrob actor turned billionaire producer who returns upstate every year to visit his family. He's shopping for a replacement gift for his mother, after accidentally leaving her Tiffany lamp at home, when he notices the lovely young mother in the inadequate coat coming his way. Caught under the mistletoe, he's startled and amused when the little girl in her arms leans over and kisses his cheek as she passes by.

Lorena and James quickly connect as the determined Cindy plays Cupid. But there's just one problem: James's meddling ex Andrea Case is using his family Christmas as a bid to get him back—and she has James's gullible mom on her side.

Lorena

All I want for Christmas is to give my little girl any Christmas at all. Since my husband Manny died in Afghanistan in a military operation that couldn't go on his record, I never received any death benefits, or even a body to bury. For two and a half years, we've been living on the edge of starvation while I work two jobs and scramble to save our house. It's been hell—and I've done everything in my power to shield my little girl from the worst of it.

But then comes the day when my baby girl leans over to kiss a random stranger under the mistletoe while I'm walking by. The stranger turns out to be *the* James Norris, a hot Hollywood producer worth more money than anyone could ever spend. And the weirdest part of all is—he's wonderful. And he likes me. When he promises me and my little girl to give us a proper Christmas after all, I wonder if I'm getting a second chance at love—and life.

James

When the prettiest young widow in the world comes walking into my life with her adorable daughter, I fall pretty damn fast.
I've put my career first for most of my life, and now that I'm past forty, I'm starting to wonder if it's time to think about all the things I sacrificed. Like having a family. Having a sweet face to

wake up to in the morning, and loving arms to fall into at night. Lorena just might be the right person to fix all of that for me.

Winning her over is going to take some work; she has a baby daughter to protect, along with her own broken heart. But that's not the complication I'm worried about. My ex, expert gold digger Andrea Case, is inserting herself into my family's Christmas celebration, manipulating my mother into making sure she can stay. Is she going to ruin Christmas? Or can I find out a way to save it for all of us?

CHAPTER 1

Lorena

Twenty dollars has never made me feel so happy. It's December 23rd and finally, after months of scrambling to keep the heat on and have food in the fridge, I have twenty dollars leftover to buy my baby daughter, Cindy, a Christmas present. It hurts to be this grateful for something so small—especially when Christmas dinner will be a cheap takeout pizza—but it's still a relief, something I haven't felt in months.

So when I walk out of the front door with my two-year-old nestled in my arms, a thick wool blanket wrapped around us both to make up for our inadequate jackets, I'm distracted enough by our good fortune that I don't notice the mistletoe at first.

Phoenicia is one of those tiny little towns in Upstate New York that survives on being pretty, having touristy shops and venues, and having the only late-night gas station for several miles. It has a bed and breakfast, a theater, a fifties-style diner, boutiques, an old German butcher, and a whole lot of drafty old

Victorians. One of those drafty Victorians was left to me in my aunt's will, so Cindy and I moved here from Long Island after my husband, Manny, died.

Getting the house was a bittersweet, survival-level stroke of luck—but a big one, with Manny's benefits tangled up in red tape for over two years. I wouldn't be so scared if it was just me, but I have our daughter to worry about too—to keep warm, sheltered, and fed. I swore on Manny's grave that I'd do my best job. Cindy is the one steady light in my life, and as usual my focus is on her more than anything else as we walk along the sidewalk—up until everything starts going weird around us.

I smell the fresh scent of cut mistletoe first—that slightly astringent smell, mixed with the slightly piney perfume of the berries. I'm used to catching whiffs of it all through the Christmas season, but as I draw near the main street, the wind picks up and blows the overpowering smell of the plant into my face.

I stop, eyes watering from the wind, and look around in confusion. The smell is so intense that it's almost like someone's burning a pile of the stuff. I look around and see no fire, but abruptly notice the sheer quantity of the stuff. Mistletoe is hanging everywhere, all over town.

Every doorway, the corners of every house and awning, the arching light displays running over the streets, the lampposts, everywhere that a sprig of mistletoe can hang, at least one dangles, hung by a red ribbon. I start moving slowly toward the closest one, not entirely sure what I'm seeing.

"Mommy, what's the smelly green stuff?" Cindy is immediately fascinated, but I gently steer her out of grabbing distance of the sprigs. The stuff is poisonous, but the berries smell nice. Bad combination around a tiny kid.

"It's mistletoe, honey. People kiss under it. See?" I point to an elderly couple smooching while a couple of Millennial girls take their picture, looking charmed. The couple is pretty cute. I wonder how many decades of marriage they have under their belt—and then I remember Manny and look away, my heart stinging.

"Oooh. Is it magic?" Cindy sounds excited. Magic is her thing. Her favorite stories are fairy tales—even the creepy ones.

"I don't know," I reply honestly. I'm that way about everything: magic, prayer, Santa, karma, God. I've always believed that any kind of religious opinion or paranormal belief should be sorted out by individuals, and not fed to them by their parents.

I also never want Cindy thinking that I know everything, or that I never make mistakes. No pedestal for me means less chance of disappointing her later—a consideration I wish my parents had given me. Not that I would ever leave my daughter to drag me to bed at night because Mommy and Daddy had too much happy juice, but still.

It's the middle of the day two days before Christmas, and of course the streets are jammed with last-minute shoppers. There's a toy store two blocks down that has plushy snowshoe hares. That's what Cindy wants: a snow bunny. Fifteen dollars plus tax, and enough change left over for a bag of Christmas candy.

Unfortunately, I'll have to push through this gawking crowd to get to our destination. It's not going to be easy—because like me, they're shocked by the sudden appearance of all this ... greenery. And that means they're mostly standing around, blocking my way.

They're either standing around talking about the mistletoe, or bustling around trying to clear it from their properties, sweeping small piles of mistletoe into the gutters—and yes, some of them are standing around kissing under it. It's very cute and kind of ridiculous, and I wonder how many people had to get together early this morning to pull this prank. Not to mention, who they were.

There's a man leaning against a lamppost on the corner as I cross the street. It takes me a moment to recognize him as Jack Whitman, a local billionaire's son and world-class skier. He's beautiful, with his pale face and coal black hair, those bright blue eyes and that deep blue overcoat. He gives me a smile and a wink as I walk past, and I blush slightly while Cindy waves at him.

I wonder what he's doing out watching all this? Is he involved? Is he behind this, maybe? He certainly does seem to be gloating a little. I glance back at him and see that he's wiggling his fingers back at Cindy, his eyes dancing with mischief and good humor. *No way of knowing.*

The Whitmans—just the father and his adult son, as far as I know—live in a giant old house far up the mountainside, and venture down to see us once every week or so. The local rich eccentrics, they are known for their grand gestures around the holidays—such as the massive food donations to the local church that I hope Dr. Whitman will make again. Last time netted each of us enough frozen and canned food to see every poor person in and around Phoenicia through to mid-January.

The elder Whitman is his son's opposite in looks, aside from them both being tall and blue-eyed. Dr. Whitman's complexion is ruddy; his features are generous. He wears a full white beard and mustache, and he always wears a cap over his bald spot, with silver hair flowing from beneath it. Nobody knows why the pair picked a tiny, sleepy town like Phoenicia to settle in, but the kids love them, and they never seem to do any harm.

If the mistletoe prank is their doing, though, this latest grand gesture is ... beyond bizarre.

"I'm cold, Mommy. Can we stop for a cocoa?" The chirpy little voice at my ear drags me back to earth. Cindy's getting big

—I'm strong, but my arm is starting to ache. Still, we only have the one wool blanket to use as a shawl, and I can't wrap it around us both if she walks beside me.

I do a quick bit of poverty math in my mind. A big cup of cocoa with whipped cream and sprinkles for each of us at the candy shop will mean temporary relief from the cold, but no Christmas candy. But I do have baking chocolate, sugar, vanilla, and milk at home.

"Can you hold out until after we get your bunny and go home? If you can wait that long, you can have two mugs of chocolate." Made from scratch, each mug costs maybe forty cents apiece.

I hate having to bargain with my baby daughter over tiny things, but I have no choice. Not even at Christmas. That's just how it is. She'll get two gifts from the toy drive that she won't get to pick, Christmas cookies because I bake them, a five-dollar pizza, one bag of chocolate drops in bright foil for her stocking, and her snow bunny. And then I'll be broke again until my next check, and praying that the Whitmans give us another break.

She lifts her head to peer at me, her dark eyes thoughtful in her round little face. She has her father's looks and his way of drawing her little brows together as she thinks something over. "All right, Mommy," she says very solemnly, and snuggles closer to me. "But hurry up!"

"I'll do my best." The sidewalks are slippery from all the slush from a recent snowfall. The shopkeepers try to sweep the worst of it back into the gutters, but I can feel my worn boot treads slide slightly every few steps. I take deep breaths and fight a surge of panic every time I slip more than half an inch, praying we won't go down in this crowd of shoppers and gawkers.

We're half a block from the toy store when I see a man step out of the tobacco shop two doors down and stop dead for a moment, my eyes widening. It's him—James Norris. Former leading man, billionaire media mogul, and the only man associated with Phoenicia who could give the mysterious Whitmans a run for their money in terms of wealth and success. I've heard before that he sometimes visit town, but I've never seen him myself.

I've had a crush on him since I hit puberty. Now in his forties, he's every bit as hot as he was back when I fell asleep next to open magazines filled with pictures of his tanned and smiling face. His thick brown hair sweeps back from a high forehead; his features are rugged and his mouth generous. His smile is like a flash of light, making his golden-hazel eyes twinkle. Only the slight crow's feet at the corners of his eyes give him away as being over thirty.

He's dressed down today in jeans, snow boots, and a thick Irish sweater in storm-cloud gray. He rocks on his heels as he checks his phone, seemingly oblivious to the gigantic bundle of mistletoe he's just stopped under. We're headed straight for him.

Oh God. For a split second I'm torn between marching up and ambushing him for a kiss that would probably warm me through the next year, and crossing the street just to avoid him. My heart bangs in my ears. I'm suddenly terribly aware of the way my pale blonde hair has slipped loose in wisps from my messy braid, of my cheap lipstick and wind-flushed cheeks.

It's the chance of a lifetime, but weird proliferation of mistletoe or not, I just can't face him.

I take the third option, walking toward him in the crowd, stepping around him politely, and pretending I don't recognize him even though my whole body feels like it's vibrating with rushes of adrenaline. I'm almost past him when I feel Cindy's weight shift. I turn around—just in time to see her lean over and lay a big kiss on James Norris's cheek.

CHAPTER 2

James

I didn't intend to go down the hill to town today. It's ridiculous, really, how I ended up wading through Phoenicia's last-minute shopping crowd while everyone else up at Mom's house had all their presents tucked under the tree already. It's my own fault, though. I managed to leave the Tiffany lamp I bought for my mother's collection sitting on my penthouse couch as I left to drive upstate.

MY DISTRACTION WAS UNDERSTANDABLE; my mother *had* just informed me that Andrea, my ex, would be staying with us for Christmas. The smartest thing that surgically-enhanced little gold digger ever did was ingratiate herself with Mom. I've been looking forward to getting away from my New York City problems for a few weeks. It irritates me to discover that one of the worst of them has followed me home for the holidays.

. . .

MOTHER HAS NEVER FORGIVEN me for breaking up with Andrea, and has tried to get me and Andrea back together more than once. She doesn't understand that Andrea is a high-maintenance gold digger who whines and nags to get her way and refuses to even contemplate having kids. Even if Andrea wasn't a bitch, she's not the one for me, and both she and my mother refuse to see that.

IN A WAY, the errand is a welcome vacation from the tension up the hill. Andrea, demanding that the heat be turned up to eighty, has spent the whole day since I showed up slinking around in a gold lamé mini dress and matching pumps, with her red hair piled artfully and hard gray eyes ringed with kohl. Clouds of musky perfume follow her around; like her artfully revealing taste in clothes, it once attracted me, but now it makes me a little sick.

I CAN'T BREATHE until I go out. Andrea refuses to go out in the cold with me, for which I'm grateful. The only part of me that still likes her is my cock, and the sway of her hips in that tight, shimmering dress had gotten my libido and me into a hell of a fight on the way out the door. It leaves me distracted and thinking of sex—and wishing I had someone kind and friendly to have a little fun with.

Andrea is a particular type of high-end sex worker who doesn't like viewing herself that way. But her brand of trophy wife isn't there to love your kids, or ease away your stress, or do much of anything besides look good on your arm, spend your money, and fuck. Like an escort. Once I realized what she was truly after—and it took me longer than I like to admit—I tried to free myself of her, but she already had her hooks sunk into my family.

D**RIVING HELPS CLEAR MY HEAD.** Early winter in New York this year was been short on snow until last week, when we got dumped on for four days straight. Now the worst of it is cleaned up enough for people to move around normally, but the whole landscape on either side of the winding mountain road is blanketed in two feet of white.

I PASS by the Whitman's Dutch revival mansion, an enormous white structure with soaring gambrel roofs, a profusion of columns, and trim in scarlet and green. Even during the day those two have enough lights and decorations that their sprawling front lawn looks like a fairy land. The local kids love it; so do I. Andrea, predictably, called it "garish," but she has all the Christmas spirit of a coal hopper.

Phoenicia has gentrified a little over the years, some of the touristy shops giving way to boutiques and specialty stores. One thing it's always been, though, is big on holidays. But when I pull onto the main street and start looking for parking, it looks just a bit like the Phoenicians have gone overboard. What is with all the mistletoe?

I'M STILL WONDERING about that a half an hour later as I step out of the tobacco shop where I've picked up an inlaid wood desk humidor for Mom's new boyfriend, Mitch. It, and the antique jewelry box I got Mom as a substitute gift, nestle in cocoons of tissue paper inside my shopping bag. I've got nothing to actually do back at Mom's place aside from making small talk and dodging Andrea, so I'm trying to come up with excuses to prolong my shopping trip.

My phone goes off as I step outside, and I sigh and reach into my pocket to check it. My mother's number. Of course. Andrea would never call herself, not when she can get my poor, gullible mom to summon me home for her.

Mom means well. She just desperately wants me settled with a houseful of cute grandkids, and Andrea has lied to her about her intentions this whole time. My mom is a very honest woman who has so little experience with lying that she can't tell when she's being led on. So Andrea uses her, and she argues in Andrea's defense in return.

I tuck the phone back into my pocket, determined to at least have a few more minutes to myself. *I'll tell her I was in the shop buying the humidor.* It's the excuse I gave for coming down here, anyway. I'm certainly not admitting to my mother that I left the lamp she's been coveting for months on my damned couch.

Fortunately, her birthday's in January, so she'll just have to wait to get it then.

Phoenicia is lovely as always. I would settle here myself if it wasn't so far from everything I'm doing. As it is, I've thought seriously about weekending over here in a house of my own. But

God, the crowds are thick today. Not that that's any surprise, given the date.

I stand out of the way as best I can, trying to ignore the sharp smell of the mistletoe hanging everywhere. Maybe I can duck into the cafe for some lunch. Or even grab a few more gifts to tuck under the tree. I'm looking up and down the street, weighing my options, when I notice a lovely young mother approaching me.

SHE'S SMALL, youthful, and almost delicate looking, with large, innocent green eyes, wispy blond hair gleaming like spun gold against her pale cheeks, and lips painted a simple pink. I can't see much of her figure under the gray wool blanket she's got wrapped around herself and her child, but that doesn't matter. I'm already charmed. Especially when I notice the lack of a wedding ring.

BEHAVE, I warn myself, though really, the lady's sweet face reminds me of how I've been longing for a little more sweetness in my life. Especially after spending the morning dealing with that bitter, gilded viper that's invaded my mother's home.

THE CHERUB she has with her is dark-haired and olive-skinned, her brown eyes full of wonder at the world as she gazes around. The two of them talk for a moment—and then the mother notices me and hesitates.

I QUICKLY PRETEND NOT to be watching her, busying myself again with my phone. I text my mother with *"in shop, call soon"* and glance up again, noticing the blonde gazing at me all wide-eyed. I've been recognized.

IT HAPPENS SOMETIMES, even though I've been behind the cameras in various capacities, instead of in front of them, for over ten years. Most people reach a certain level of stardom and wealth and blow it on a lavish lifestyle, drugs, friends, what have you. I invested it, determined to create a production company where I could create good movies without tripping over corporate politics.

THINGS TURNED out better than expected. So I've been out of the spotlight for a while, at least on that level. I'm the man behind the curtain now.

BUT NOT TO THIS ONE. I see the old dazzle in her eyes for a moment, and then the most charming attack of shyness that I have ever witnessed. For a moment I wonder if she's going to walk up to me, or run away. I'm disappointed when she lowers her gaze and moves to walk around me instead.

Then the little cherub in her arms, mischief in her eyes, leans over and lays a smooch right on my cheek!

THE POOR WOMAN FREEZES, her eyes flying wide open again, and looks up at me in a panic. I let out a laugh, even more charmed than before, and glance up at the bundle of mistletoe hanging directly over my head. "And a merry Christmas to you too," I inform the little girl, who is grinning hugely.

. . .

"Oh my God," the woman mumbles in such a mortified tone that I want to pat her shoulder and tell her it's okay. I mind her personal space, though, and just maintain my smile and shake my head.

"It's no trouble. She caught me fair and square!" I give the woman a smile, and she starts to relax, seeming a little baffled that this is actually happening. *Poor thing. It's all right, dear, I'm not going to bite!*
Unless you want me to, of course.

There was a time in my career when that starry-eyed look coming from a beautiful young woman would have had me angling to get her into bed. With fans, it's generally fairly easy—and fun for all, at least when I do it. Looking at her and at the soft light in her eyes when she gazes up at me, I'm tempted to do it again.

"Yes, I did catch you," the little one insists, and then says firmly, "And that means you owe me and Mommy a cocoa! The kind with the whipped cream and peppermint sticks!" She even pokes a finger into my chest.

The poor woman. It's all I can do not to laugh as she gives her opportunistic child a look of horror. "I—I'm sorry," she starts, but I just smile and shake my head.

"Don't you worry about any of that. I'm charmed, and fortunately for us all, I could really use the distraction." I gaze down at her as she stares up at me, still slightly starry-eyed. Her little girl is beaming with such deep self-satisfaction that I almost start laughing again. This kid really knows what she's doing.

"My name's James," I say warmly, never breaking the woman's gaze. I've missed having someone look up at me like I hung the moon, especially after Andrea's hot-cold mix of manipulative sweetness and disdain. There's nothing manipulative about this woman. "What's yours?"

"Lorena," she murmurs tentatively, as if she's worried I might be playing a prank on her. "This is Cindy."

"Well, pleased to meet you both," I reply, before gesturing toward the cafe. "Now let's all get a hot drink, shall we?"

CHAPTER 3

Lorena

When we walk in the door of the chrome-countered, checker-floored café, I still don't know whether to reprimand Cindy or thank her. Never in my life would I have dreamed that a man like James Norris would end up taking me out for cocoa, but here he is, holding the door for us.

I set Cindy down with a sigh now that we're out of the cold, and roll my throbbing shoulder before removing the blanket and draping it over one arm. She waits beside me patiently, looking around at everything but staying quiet. I take her hand again and we follow the waitress to a table. James pulls out my chair.

As I'm sitting down, my mind's eye suddenly conjures Manny sliding into the seat across from me as I scoot in unassisted. He was young and artless, but devoted—the kind of romantic who had trouble expressing it. He forgot to pull out chairs. I wince slightly, and hide my expression by quickly snatching up a drinks menu.

"Clever of them to sell hot drinks in all these different flavors when it's this cold out," James comments as he sits down. He towers over me, even when sitting—a giant compared to me and Cindy. "I understand that Miss Cindy likes the peppermint cocoa. Do you have a preference?"

He's leaning toward me, his voice a deep, friendly purr, and my heartbeat suddenly pounds in my ears. I can't catch my breath. I can smell his musky cologne, and the faint scent of mistletoe still hanging around him. "I ..." I force out, and then look hurriedly down at the menu.

Maybe I should have just kissed him and been done with it. It can't end up more awkward than this.

"I've never had most of these," I admit finally, in a soft, hesitant voice. If we ever go for a treat, I get a cup of something very plain and let Cindy revel in her whipped cream-covered delight. I've never even *heard* of most of these drinks.

"Well, what appeals?" he asks without missing a beat.

I look down the list and pick one, a little desperate to avoid trying his patience. "Um ... maybe the salted caramel?"

"Salted caramel it is. Clearly you need a treat too, after carrying such a big girl around all by yourself." His eyes dance even more in person than they used to in my magazines. His charisma pulls at me like a magnet. I might have had a crush on him before, but right now, as I bask in the light of his smile, I forget every one of my problems all at once.

How does he do that?

He orders two salted caramel mochas and peppermint hot cocoa, all in their biggest size, and a plate of fruit turnovers to share. Cindy bounces happily at the prospect, and I have to admit my mouth waters a little too. I can bake pastries, but unless I have a lull between my jobs there's no time to do so.

Immediately after the smiling waitress walks away, his phone rings. "Ah, sorry," he says, fishing his phone from his jeans pocket and checking it. He frowns. "It's family. Please give me a moment."

He turns partially away before putting his phone to his ear. "Yes, hi Mom." A pause. His smile starts to look a little forced. "No, I ran into a friend in the tobacco shop, and we're having a hot drink before I drive back up."

I try to distract myself by looking around, but I'm dead curious, and find myself listening in regardless. There's a certain amount of tension to the long pause that follows as his mother talks, as if he's listening to a lecture. "Mom, look, I understand that she invited herself to Christmas, but that is between Andrea and you. She and I haven't had a relationship in several months."

My ears prick up. *What?*

James has been linked for years to the notoriously high-maintenance model-actress Andrea Case. He has never been seen in public with anyone else. But apparently, all of that came to an end earlier this year, while I was too wrapped up in hustling to pay my bills to keep tabs.

"Mom, please don't let Andrea push you around like that. It's bad enough that she invited herself over for Christmas. This is your home, and I came to visit you. Not her. If she can't handle my leaving for a while, she can always come join me."

The corner of his mouth curls knowingly; Andrea doesn't seem the type to brave the snowy streets of Phoenicia, and it seems that he's counting on that.

So Andrea is still following him around even though he's told everyone that they are quits. She apparently is conning his mom and is trying to control him. And he's just trying to come down here for a little break or something, but Andrea won't even allow that. I have a nose for putting stories together, and this one has me intrigued.

"Don't let her worry you, Mom, it's fine. I'll be back soon."

He hangs up and puts his phone away, giving me an apologetic look. "Sorry. Family holiday ... things, you know how it is."

"Not really," I reply honestly, which gets me a sharply curious look. "It's just me and my little one here. My husband died two years ago on deployment."

He blinks in surprise, and his gaze sweeps over us again. I brace myself; he's taking in the thin puffer jackets we're wearing, the wool blanket we were using as a shawl, the careful patch in my shoulder bag. I have nothing to be ashamed of; I'm a good person in bad circumstances, and I'm doing the best I can.

But ... what wealthy man ever sees it that way? Aside from Dr. Whitman and his son, of course. But even they're considered eccentric—exceptions that prove the rule. This man, James, whom I've daydreamed about since I was twelve, has no reason to sympathize. No reason not to dismiss me as cheap, lazy, and just a step above a beggar—if that.

My cheeks burn and my eyes sting alarmingly. My stomach shivers with a mix of humiliation and dread. How will he react?

"Ah, well then. That's unfortunate. I thought perhaps that you were here to see relatives." He seems to want to say more for a moment, but then sits back and smiles at the waitress as she brings our drinks. He seems a little relieved by the interruption.

I'm more than relieved. Though after a moment, I realize that the look on his face is more concerned than anything. I push the conversation on to what I hope is more comfortable territory. "So, you're visiting family?"

I know his mother lives in the area. Every local who follows the movie industry at all knows that. But it seems rude to just assume, as if I know about him from anything besides online gossip articles.

"Oh yes," he says, perking up. "My brothers and I visit my mother every year and stay for a few weeks. She's a bit like the

Whitmans—she goes mad for Christmas and everything to do with it. Her house looks like a parade float right now."

"That makes me smile. "That's adorable." My own house, well ... I just can't afford Christmas lights. We have a tiny tree in the front yard that we trim with peanuts and popcorn and let the birds and squirrels eat, only to string up more the next day. But at night, there's nothing in my yard but darkness.

"I'm sorry if I've brought up something that is uncomfortable for you," he says quietly as he slides our drinks to us. They are each in a huge mug, with a small mountain of whipped cream on top. Cindy's has a candy cane stuck into it, which she eagerly pulls out and starts using like a dipping stick. I make sure I have extra napkins handy for her before turning back to him.

"It's not like that. We haven't been on our own very long, and I'm still getting used to Christmases alone." That part's true.

Even back when my parents were too busy drinking to do anything, my Aunt Erin would always take over, making sure that I had something to celebrate, at least for a few days. After she passed away, I had one Christmas with Manny before he shipped out. And now it's been two bleak years of Cindy and I fending for ourselves.

I just wish I could give her a better life than this. Cindy is as happy and content as I can manage. Fortunately she's not a demanding kid. But when she gets older, when she's in school, having a poor single mom will weigh against her socially, just as it weighs against me now.

I don't really have many friends in town. Clients, sure. Nobody has a problem with me doing their books, cleaning their houses, or looking after their pets. They will share a church pew with me, a bus seat, or the counter at the cafe. They just have a problem with being seen with me in any situation where we might be taken for ... peers.

Even now, I can see the curious looks from locals and shoppers as they see the three of us together; the plain, slightly ragged girl, her adorable but inadequately dressed kid, and the billionaire superstar. I know what some of them must be thinking: *what's he doing with her?* And it makes me feel a little better, like I'm thumbing my nose at their stupid prejudice.

Relying on charity upstate, regardless of your run of bad luck, wins you no friends, even when you're a war widow. But James isn't from upstate. And as I notice he's still listening to me and has made no move to leave, I really start to relax.

"Well, that's rather sad. And you live in town, then?" He spoons aside some of his cream to keep it from getting on his nose as he takes a swallow of his drink. "Mm. That's divine. Really, Lorena, you should try this."

I hesitate. It smells decadent enough to make my mouth water, as does the scent of the pastries. I wanted to save it a moment longer, but I need the distraction from the awkward topic.

I scoop up the long spoon and nip up a mix of foam, cream, and caramel drizzle on the end of it. I slide it into my mouth ... suddenly aware of how closely he's watching. I lick the spoon clean, the unbelievable mix of rich sweetness and subtle shifts of flavor melting on my tongue. Then I swallow, taking a little gasp of breath in surprise. "Wow."

His smile widens again. "See?"

"I need help Mommy!" Cindy announces, and I turn at once to help her hold the big mug and avoid getting cream all over her face. She laughs as she gets a little gob on her nose. I hear James chuckling warmly beside us.

I turn back to him and see him looking at us with something I would never have expected. Not pity or amusement, not mockery or barely hidden disdain, but rather ... wistfulness. His eyes are sad, with the warm, longing look of a dog staring after his family's car.

"What is it?" I ask him gently, suddenly too arrested by his unspoken sadness to care much whether I make a bad impression.

"I'm sorry, I just ... your family may be small, but there's real warmth there. That's rarer than it should be." He tilts his head slightly. "So, what do you do for work?"

I squash a moment of defensive nervousness and answer the question directly. "A bit of everything. I've got a client who I'm a personal attendant for, another one I shop for. I take in packages for a dozen people around town and walk several people's dogs. I house sit in the off-season. Things like that."

I wish I could describe my scramble to get enough work in half a dozen fields as something more glamorous, or at least difficult. But the real problem is cramming in enough hours of such work to make ends meet. Rich people don't stay rich by being generous with the help.

His eyebrows rise. "Oh. Well, you know, if you have a card or something, my mother's been looking for a companion. She's in good health, but she doesn't drive, and she spends too much time up on that mountain eating out of cans."

My heart jumps. I don't care that it's not the kind of relationship I wish I could have with the man. It's the possibility of a solid job with a client whose refreshingly non-classist son seems to like me. "I—of course. Just give me a moment."

I'm fishing for a card in the bottom of my bag, wishing I had slipped more into my wallet, when Cindy drops her spoon. "Need more help, Mommy!"

"Just a minute, hun," I say distractedly as I dig. *Of all the times I've carried these cards around and not needed one, now I need one and can't find it.*

"Here, let me help." James quickly moves to offer his own spoon, and Cindy takes it and happily keeps eating the cream off the top of her cocoa.

"Thank you," I say as I finally find one of my simple business cards and hand it over to him. He accepts it, and I settle back to take a swallow of my own drink.

I try to savor it. It's not just a drink—it's a dessert. This and the turnovers are probably the only real treats I'll get this holiday. Soon, though, if this client comes through, I'll be able to afford treats now and again once more.

"So what kind of help would your mother need?" It's an easy topic to jump into.

"Besides driving into town and occasionally going to doctor's appointments, she spends late winter in Florida and will need a sitter for her house and cats. It's not difficult work; she already has a maid. And she loves kids, so you could probably bring the little princess along." He winks at Cindy, who looks back at him solemnly.

I fight down a laugh at my daughter's deepening frown. "Uh oh. Now you've done it."

Cindy folds her arms. "I'm not a princess. I'm a vampire."

"Oh, I'm terribly sorry, my mistake." James puts a hand on his broad chest and I'm all blushes and stifled giggles again, watching. He gives her a confused look. "But if that's so, how can you drink cocoa?"

"Cocoa's yummy. Dracula doesn't drink wine cause he wanted cocoa." She carefully lifts the mug in both hands and takes a wobbly swallow, only spilling a little. I swoop in with a napkin before the droplets can run down her chin.

James is very good with her, I think. At least, from what I've seen so far. He also seems very attentive to my moods and needs, which is rare, especially in a stranger.

Is he putting on an act to impress me for some reason? Or is he sincere, and just better at showing it than many?

I realize that not even Manny was this attentive. Manny, who left a hole in my heart the exact shape of his memory, was a soldier, not a gentleman. Quiet, stoic, who prayed more often than he drank, was shy in bed and yet loving, and spent every minute of his life with me that his military commission allowed.

I loved him. I miss him. But he never had a tenth of the charm of the man across the table from me.

It's been two years and change since I've let a man touch me—since I've even wanted a man to touch me. It's only ever been Manny. Movie-star crushes are just a way of letting off steam.

Until they're in front of you, flesh and blood, friendly and charming as hell, and the possibility of actually going to bed with them becomes a faint blip on the horizon.

Why else would he be so friendly? Is he just horny, or lonely for someone who won't treat him like this Andrea woman seems to? The idea of his being lonely is a slippery slope by itself. It makes my heart open a crack—and with that comes a surge of guilt, because the man I'm feeling that bit of tenderness toward is not my husband.

To this day, I'll never know what secret assignment Manny was on that left him and half his squad dead, with mourning families trapped in the same red-tape nightmare as I. Four of us wives have no bodies to bury, no explanations of what happened. Nothing to show for our loved ones but the government sending empty letters with official words instead of any consideration, financial or otherwise.

How can these men's service not be acknowledged just because the specifics of their mission have to be kept secret? No one has ever had an answer for us. We've been struggling with the help of volunteer attorneys for over eighteen months to get them. But the Veterans Administration has not budged.

The other widows and I still keep in touch. We have an email chain that we share legal information and news on, and chat together. Awkward pen pals scattered across the state, reaching out to each other now and again when the pressure gets to be too much and no one else can understand. It is like having four sisters—sisters in blood.

"I think I could do all of that for her easily. How many hours a day would she need me?" I am praying that his mother will need me a lot. Almost everything else I do can be shuffled around or done on the way to completing other errands. But a solid job where I can bring my daughter? *Where do I sign up?*

"I'll talk to my mother and call you with details," he says brightly as he enters my number into his cellphone. "It won't be more than a day or two."

"Thank you," I murmur, still shocked at the sudden opportunity.

"Oh, don't thank me. I haven't actually had an uninterrupted chat with someone so pleasant since I got here." He winks. "So perhaps I have a few ulterior motives in recommending you."

"O-oh," I murmur, blinking, my heart pounding again. Cindy takes one look at my blushing face and starts giggling.

CHAPTER 4

James

It amazes me how much better I feel after just that short interaction with lovely, good-hearted Lorena and her daughter. I very rarely feel a spark this strong with anyone, and with a tiny bit of a star-struck crush shining in her eyes, Lorena's almost irresistible. In other circumstances, I would have canceled everything and suggested that she and I spend a few days exploring this attraction.

I will have to be patient, though. Single mom, desperate circumstances, and me with an unwanted ex hanging around—it's not a great situation to be in to try to get acquainted. And Lorena appears to be the shy type—which is charming, but also means it's best to go slowly with her.

I hope Mom likes the idea of hiring her. I want to help Lorena without hurting her pride. I caught sight of those too-thin jackets and inadequate boots. They were using a military blanket as a shawl to share. I could fix many of those problems just with the contents of my wallet, but I want to be able to do it in a way that's lasting, in a way that will help her help herself. Gentle-hearted single moms still have their pride.

Besides, it will be an excuse to have her around. And from the lightness I feel even as I walk up the front steps of Mom's towering blue Victorian, having her around will be a very good thing for me as well as her. I'm humming to myself as I unlock the garland-draped front door and step inside.

"Oh, what did you get?" My mother greets me at the door, all smiles, and I have to gently keep her from poking into my shopping bags. She's a tiny, chubby woman, whose face has that sweet Italian apple-doll look to it, her eyes magnified by big round glasses. "Come on, let me take a peek!"

"No, no, come on now, I got some last-minute stocking stuffers for all of you and I don't want to ruin the surprise." I give her a kiss on the top of the head as I bundle past into the hallway.

"Oh, all right. I just wanted to see what you got Mitch!" She trails after me as I make my way to the first-floor bedroom I'm staying in for the week.

"All right, all right, let's go in my room and I'll show you." I need to get there anyway. The warm air stings my chilled skin comfortingly, but I know I'll need to change out of my sweater in a few minutes. Andrea's diva insistence on hothouse temperatures will cook me alive otherwise.

I step up to the door and push it open—and see Andrea waiting for me on my bed.

In gold lingerie, the mini-dress draped over my bedside chair, the gleaming silk teddy clinging to her robust curves. My idiot body reacts instinctively to the display. Right in front of my mother.

There's a long, awkward pause as we stare at each other. Her seductive smile melts as I watch, as if it's suddenly dawning on her that it's the middle of the afternoon in a busy household and

I might not be coming in alone. My poor mom, meanwhile, gapes next to me like she's just walked in on the two of us fucking.

"I think you're in the wrong room," I say conversationally.

Andrea blinks at me, and then sputters, "What the hell are you doing?" as if it isn't somehow obvious.

"Well, I'm coming in with my mom to wrap the gifts I just bought. What the hell are *you* doing?" God, this scheming idiot. Not only does she ignore my comfort level and try to use me, but she does the exact same thing to my poor mother. *I have to put a stop to this.*

"Oh, dear. I .... um ..." Mom flaps her hands slightly and I turn to her at once, ushering her out of the room.

"It's all right. She's clearly drunk, so we'll just leave her alone to pull herself together. We'll use the breakfast nook," I insist softly, and she nods, blushing to the roots of her white hair.

I shoot Andrea a glare over my shoulder. "Get out of my room. I'm keeping this door locked from now on."

Andrea's jaw drops and then she glares. She starts saying something snippy, but I ignore her and get Mom down the stairs, into the kitchen, and over to a seat in the big, octagonal breakfast nook.

"She's just trying to repair your relationship," my mother says weakly. But it's clear that this time, Andrea has made her uncomfortable too. Were I nastier, I would probably say something about how she brought this on herself. As it is, I'm hoping this is the shock Mom needs to stop trusting my meddling ex.

"Mom," I say quietly as I set the bags on the table and sit down across from her, "I know that you like Andrea and that you consider her a friend. But she's also not the person that you think she is. I'm sorry." I reach over and squeeze her chubby little hand, and wonder when she got so small and delicate. "We don't have a relationship anymore, because we want two entirely different things out of a relationship."

Also, she's a horrifying bitch, and if I ever raised my hand to a woman it would be to toss her out of this house by the scruff like a bad dog.

She shakes her head. "She really wants to be with you, Jamie, she means it."

"She does want to be with me. That much is true. And it's also true that we were good together for a little while. But we're just not compatible, and I don't want to be with her. She doesn't love me; she doesn't want kids; and she uses people. Me, you, anyone she can get her hands on." I look at her sincerely, and she sighs and looks down.

"If she doesn't love you," she murmurs, "if she just wants your money like you keep saying, then why would she try so hard to have you?"

"Because she doesn't know when to give up, Mom. She hates losing, she hates being told no, and she hates being kept from having things she wants." *And I hate having to have this conversation. I'm so sorry, Mom.*

She's starting to look upset, so I reach into one of the bags and pull out the humidor, some tape, and a package of wrapping paper.

"Let's take a break from dwelling on this mess. We'll sort out what to do when emotions aren't so high. Look here." I unwrap the humidor, which is cedar inlaid with cocobolo and ebony. "This is what I got Mitch. Do you think he'll like it?"

Her face lights up and I can see the relief in her eyes that I don't plan to let these problems with Andrea ruin our Christmas. "Oh, that's lovely. You know, I don't think he has a humidor."

"Well, I know he likes cigars, and they're no fun when they dry out and die." I start wrapping as we talk.

This is how Mom has been ever since my father died. The shock of losing her best friend of fifty years took something away from her besides just her spouse. She has a certain fragility now that she never had before. Too much conflict or stress and she wilts, sometimes taking to bed like a Victorian lady with weak nerves. I've learned to understand her limits and work with them.

Andrea, on the other hand, doesn't give a damn. She'll use and hurt my mother just like she tried to do to me, and blame both of us if she doesn't get exactly what she wants, exactly when she wants it. And that right there is part of why she will never be right for me, ever.

We're talking as I wrap everything from my bags that isn't meant for Mom. I keep the jewelry box and the Tiffany earrings I bought to put in it hidden. My middle brother Aaron has a carsick four-year-old and will be a little late, she tells me. Mitch has decided last minute that he wants to do a turducken for Christmas dinner. I laugh at the whole idea and promise Mom that I'll help him.

I notice pretty soon after I get Mom calmed down that Andrea is hovering at the kitchen door, arms folded, staring at me. She's out of my mother's line of sight, which I'm grateful for because she's making things more awkward by the minute. I keep talking about cheerful, mundane things, ignoring her.

"Anyway, while I was in town my friend gave me a reference to someone who works as a companion and errand-runner. You said you were looking to hire an assistant."

I cross my fingers mentally, watching from the corner of my eye as Andrea frowns and unfolds her arms, a line appearing between her brows. *That's right, you're not worth fretting over for more than five minutes at a time. We have lives to get on with.*

My mother bobs her head as she gets up to put the teapot

on. "Oh yes," she says cheerfully. "I hope it's a young woman. I'd feel strange having another man in the house."

"She's a young single mother who has been working up here for a few years now. She needs the work, and I know you like kids, so when I found out about her I got her contact information." I offer her the card that Lorena gave me. I already have her number in my phone in case it gets lost.

"That sounds promising. Do you know what she's like? As a person, I mean." She bustles around filling a tea ball with chamomile flowers, as Andrea slowly draws back out of the doorway, apparently satisfied that we're not plotting to boot her out in the snow. *Yet.*

"She's very kind, and her little girl is almost three and an absolute sweetheart. She's a war widow." I know that will get to my mother. Maybe it's manipulative of me, but if it ends up with her getting some help and Lorena getting a job, I'll live with that mild guilt.

"Oh, well then, certainly. Let's give her a call tomorrow, once I've slept on the idea. I'm sure she won't mind a Christmas Eve call if she's hurting for work." She brings out the honey pot and turns her back to keep puttering as I surreptitiously start wrapping her gifts behind the screen of the bags.

"Just so. I hope it's a good fit." For more reasons than one.

Andrea ambushes me after dinner as I'm trying to clear my head over a brandy in Dad's old library. This time she has the sense not to barge into the room—but she doesn't knock before pushing the door open either.

I ignore her for a moment, staring into the small fire I've gotten going in the grate as I think wistfully of Lorena's shy smile. If only she were here, and not this shrew in model's clothing.

"You're being incredibly rude today," she growls from the doorway.

I take a swallow from my brandy and look up. "You have lied to and used my mother to barge in on our holiday celebration in an attempt to regain access to my wallet, you gilded vulture. You also just embarrassed the hell out of my mother and me with that cheap ladies' mag style seduction attempt.

"I don't owe you politeness. In fact, I wish you'd fuck off back to New York City and go back to snorting coke with your boy-toys."

Our eyes lock. I can see the rage in hers, and know that I've stepped over a line—but I just don't give a damn any more. I'm tired of her bullshit, her thoughtless selfishness, and her manipulative whining.

"I can't believe that you think that you can talk to me this way," she says breathlessly. "All I want is—"

"All you want is a rich husband, and you're not exactly being subtle about that. I am not what you are looking for. I'm not interested in a trophy wife. There are plenty of men who are, and some are more successful than I."

I'm keeping as calm as I can, and for a moment she actually seems to be considering this idea. I press on, gentling my tone, trying one last time for reason. "Look, in all honesty, you really shouldn't waste your time and attention on me. I'm sure a good number of wealthy men would be happy to have you." *And would never listen to you long enough to realize what a shrew you are. Go find some dumb, shallow ass looking for a hot young thing, and leave me be.*

I take another swallow of my brandy. My attempt at diplomacy, when what I really want to do is take her to pieces verbally, wears on me. *Yes, I would practically kill to have Lorena here in her place. I barely know the girl, and I already know that.*

Unfortunately Andrea's brief moment of clarity passes, and she falls back into her perpetual role of seducer, lips curving in a sly smile. "It's you I want," she purrs, slinking over, and I roll my eyes so hard that they ache. This time not even my dick is interested, even when she stands over me to give me a face full of her cleavage. "And I'm used to getting what I want."

Instead of seeing Andrea, I see Lorena's smile in my mind, her innocence, her courage in the face of exhausting effort and rough odds. We only spent an hour together talking, but it was enough time for me to know that she is far more my type than Andrea.

"Not this time," I rasp, breathing through my mouth so Andrea's perfume won't overwhelm me.

"Aww." She runs a ruby-tipped finger over my shoulder through my turtleneck, and I pull away. "Now, don't be difficult. You don't know what's good for you."

"Don't patronize me," I growl, but she just smiles lazily. I down the rest of my drink and get up, moving away from her. She follows. "This is reaching the point of stalking, Andrea."

"Stalking?" She stops dead, laughing incredulously. "Do I make you feel threatened or something? Poor baby!"

Back when her opinion meant something to me, that would have stung like hell. But the little twinge I feel now is easy to push past. "Threatened? You are ruining my holiday with my family because I won't get back together with you. I don't know how much clearer I can be that I am not interested in anything with you. I'm starting to think I'll need a restraining order to keep you at bay."

I hate myself a little for being so nasty back, but it does the trick. She backs off, eyes wide with shock. She never expects much resistance from anyone, which makes her obsession with my stubborn ass that much more baffling.

She simply doesn't seem to be smart enough to understand that she's never going to win this one. She can't get it through her head that making a mess of things for me won't attract me back to her side. *Ugh, what did I see in her?*

She lifts her chin, lips wobbly and eyes bright, and then says in a snotty voice, "What you don't understand is that I'm your best option. I have the connections. I can help you build your fortune, or I can ruin you."

"No, you can't," I reply tiredly. I'm a billionaire producer with influential friends in multiple industries across the world. She's a washed-up model who lost her shot at supermodel stardom because she was too fucking difficult for anyone to work with.

These days she can only manipulate people who are too trusting, like my mother. But every rich man in Hollywood seasoned enough to know the type, or connected enough to know her story, knows to avoid Andrea. She can't use her body to drive her point home as well as she once did.

I was at a low point, lonely and distracted by tireless work, when she attached herself to me. Now she keeps clinging on, an angry parasite fighting to reattach. "Andrea, please. Stop embarrassing everyone, stop lying to my mother, and go home."

She shakes her head as she withdraws from the room. "This isn't over."

"Yes, it very much is." I look down at my glass and drain the rest of the contents—then pour myself two fingers more. It's going to be a long night.

CHAPTER 5

Lorena

Cindy's sugar high from her afternoon feast of cocoa and apple turnovers lasts for a solid four hours. I end up chasing her around our snowy yard, building a snow dragon, and making snow angels until we're both exhausted and starved.

Homemade crockpot chicken soup stretched with vegetables is a little plain after such a gorgeous snack, but neither of us mind. She devours two bowls and watches three hours of Christmas specials before she finally runs out of steam. I eat a bowl of it, clean up from dinner, and get a little work done.

I rewrite one of my client's budgets, mend one of Cindy's dresses, and clean up the kitchen. I sit with her now and again as she watches TV, and we cuddle on the couch under our one good blanket as I stare at the screen, but see James's smile and hear his voice. I'm stuck on the man, and it would feel nice if I didn't feel vaguely guilty about it.

When Cindy drowses off for good, I carry her to bed and go back to work.

My daughter is sound asleep and the house is locked up carefully by the time I settle in for a bit of me-time with my stack of library books. I'm catching up on Dean Koontz as fast as interlibrary loans can get the books to me. They're like popcorn—a little bland and repetitive, but you really can't have just one.

My room is getting chilly. To save fuel, I turn the heat down to sixty at night and give Cindy the space heater, relying on flannel and down to keep myself warm in my aunt's high, ridiculously bouncy, iron-framed bed. Right now, my toes are toasty, but the end of my nose feels like I've got my head inside my fridge.

The big, creaky house feels a little spooky at night. We've sealed the insides of all the windows with plastic to keep the heat in, and the drafts pull at them futilely, making tiny crackling noises and pushing at the curtains like ghosts. Downstairs, all the lights are off, with just the hall light and my bedside light cutting the gloom.

It's the darkest time of the year. Ironically, Cindy's not afraid of the dark at all—but I am. The dark, the cold, the emptiness. Winter's a bad time for me.

I nearly levitate off the bed when my phone rings.

I answer at once, worried that the sound will wake Cindy. She's a deep sleeper, but still. "Hello?"

"Miss Lorena? I'm sorry to bother you at this late hour, but I have an odd favor to ask." It takes me a few moments before I realize that it's *James* on the other end. "Is this a bad time?"

"I, uh—" *Oh God, wait, what's going on?* I feel a little disoriented, and have to check the lettering in my book to make certain I'm not dreaming. "No, no, it's fine. I was just doing some reading. What's the favor?"

"Well, it's abrupt, but I was just wondering if you'd like to come out and have a drink with me." His voice is strained, with that strange note I recognize from when he spoke about the warmth in my small family. There's that sadness behind it again, and I can't resist it—any more than I can resist the idea of seeing him again.

"I can't leave my daughter." I hesitate. I normally wouldn't let a man I don't know well into my home with my sleeping daughter, in the middle of the night. But ... "I don't have much here, but if you want to come over?"

A pause. "Sure. What's the address?"

I tell him and we hang up, and then the real work starts—trying to get ready to welcome a billionaire into my humble home. I draw the line at getting dressed again. It's too cold; I'm too tired; and the purple, fuzzy robe is actually the newest piece of clothing I own. But I do hustle around the living room, picking up toys and books, grabbing a stack of papers off the coffee tables and straightening the blue blankets covering both of our couches.

I kick the heat back up to seventy for now, and hear the boiler rumble to life in the basement. The heat registers tick as they come on, and I sigh with relief as the first wave of warm air wafts through the living room.

I hear his soft knock at the front door a few minutes later.

It's started snowing again, I notice as he comes in trailed by a blast of cold air. He brushes flakes off the shoulders of his forest green parka and then starts taking it off, smiling down at me tiredly. "Thanks for having me. I really needed saner company than I'm dealing with back home."

"I'll make us some tea." I point him at the tiny coat closet, and turn to go put my battered red enamel kettle on. It came with the house, just like the furniture, the linens, and all the cabinets and drawers full of my aunt's knickknacks that I'm still going through. I'm just filling the pot and lighting the aging burner with a match when he pokes his head in.

"Hi," I greet him calmly, though it's a little alarming that he suddenly seems almost desperate for my company. "Peppermint all right?"

"That's fine." He walks over to one of the mismatched, padded chairs I set around our breakfast nook table, the old wood creaking under him. "Seriously, thanks for having me."

"What happened? If you feel like talking about it, I mean." I speak carefully, not sure what I'm inviting him to unload.

He sighs. "The short version is that my ex has spent the entire evening driving me crazy, embarrassing my mother, and making one brother glad that he's married and the other glad that he's gay." He snorts. "Plus, my sister-in-law hates her as much as I do, but blames me for Andrea being around."

I wince. I don't normally get into strangers' problems, since I can barely carry my own, but it doesn't mean I don't care. If anything, I usually care too much. "So you called me so late because this is the first chance you had to slip out?"

He shakes his head. "I was trying to just get through the evening. But she decided to try to pick the lock on my bedroom door so she could slip into my bed and seduce me."

"That's ... crazy. She was actually out there with a hairpin or something?" *Who is this woman?*

"Credit card. She kept at it for twenty minutes and I just gave up trying to sleep and left." His expression softens then, those gorgeous eyes gazing into mine hypnotically. "I'm sorry I couldn't get away sooner, honestly. Somehow I think you'd have been better company this evening."

A sound comes out of my mouth that's something between a scoff and a laugh, my cheeks prickling with heat. *Oh boy.* "I spent my afternoon and evening chasing my kid around between work errands. She was flying on sugar. I think she left footprints on the ceiling in places."

He laughs, the tensions slowly clearing from his face. "See? Much better company. I can already tell."

That surprises me. Most men I have met, except for Manny and his dad, are indifferent at best when it comes to sugar-crazy two-year-olds. *But liking kids and having patience with them is also a good sign*, I catch myself thinking.

Wait. A good sign of what? This guy doesn't have any interest in me besides being friendly and getting his mom some good help. There's no way he's ... interested.

Except here he is in the middle of the night waiting patiently while I scrape the bottom of my box of peppermint tea, telling me that he's here because he needs the company of someone who is nothing like his apparently shrewish ex. How can I ignore that?

And if he *is* interested, how can I resist?

Manny. The surge of guilt nearly makes me spill the tea. Were he alive, I would never cheat. But it's been two years. I'm lonely. And apparently, so is James.

My hands shake a little as the idea of moving on rolls into my head for the first time since Manny's death. It's this girlish crush. It's making me stupid. He hasn't actually said anything about being interested in me sexually or romantically, so I shouldn't assume.

But what if he is interested?

My toes curl inside my slippers and I clumsily manage to finish putting the tea together. I can feel his eyes on me the whole time. I glance back through the archway into the living room and see that he's moved, with him now sitting on my shabby couch with his legs crossed, eyes focused on me thoughtfully. *What does he want?*

"Did you want to tell me what happened?" I ask as I bring him his mug of tea. Our fingers brush as he takes it, and it's all I can do not to drop it in his lap. *Oh boy.* "I mean, I'd probably make a crappy bartender, but you don't usually see people going out in a snowstorm to hang out with a near stranger and avoid their family."

"Not my family. Just my ex." He sighs. "Andrea might be the perfect arm candy for the paparazzi, but she's just not my type, and she doesn't get that."

He watches as I sit on the couch across from him. "And worse, she's decided to manipulate my mother into helping her get access to me. My mother just wants to see me settled, and Andrea knows just how to take advantage of that. That is the whole reason she was able to butt in on our Christmas."

"That sounds horrible." It does, though I'm a little surprised that he doesn't just tell Andrea to step off and leave his family alone. Maybe her manipulation of his mom prevents that. If she needs an assistant, she might not have the energy to devote to fending off that kind of family drama. "I don't get why she still thinks that she has a shot, though."

"Most men in my position don't marry for love. We find someone beautiful and basically use her for sex, connections, and to make us look good—in exchange, they get access to our fortunes. She expected the same from me, and she doesn't understand that I'm not into it." He gives me a small, tight smile and then takes a sip of tea. "Mm, this isn't bad. What brand?"

"I grew it." Making the backyard into a working vegetable and herb garden took me two years, thanks to my lack of time. The things that have really flourished so far besides the native chicory are the mint plants.

Peppermint for the stomach. Spearmint and chocolate mint for flavoring. Catnip for nerves, and because Cindy gets so excited when there's a kitty in the yard.

If Manny's money finally comes through for us, I'm getting her a pair of kittens. Until then, her snow bunny is wrapped in the Sunday comics and waiting by the hearth.

He blinks in surprise and smiles. "It's lovely. Good and

strong, no chemicals. So you've got a garden going? My mother wants one but has a bit of a black thumb."

"I can help her there." I take a swallow of my tea, and then add in a bit of the last of our honey. I move carefully, handling the raw local honey like gold; the jar was a gift, and I don't know when I can replace it. "Did she express any interest in having me work for her?"

"A great deal, actually." He takes another generous swallow of the mint tea and smiles thoughtfully. "No cat allergies, right?"

"No. I like them, and Cindy adores them." The neutral subject seems to be calming him down; he's relaxing, smiling more. *Or maybe it's the company.*

And maybe I shouldn't punish myself just for speculating on that. *Can't a girl dream a little?* "I'd have to get a look at your land to tell what will grow in the yard, and what would need to be grown in frames or pots and brought inside in winter."

"That's lovely. I'm sure this will work out." He fingers his mug for a moment—a big blue ceramic whale with the tail forming the handle, part of my aunt's eccentric collection. "Don't suppose you've ever handled an eviction of an unwanted guest?"

I let out an awkward laugh. "Um, well, that's the part I can't understand. Does your mother like her so much that she will just let her stay even if she's causing problems?"

He chuckles and lowers his head, his smile looking a lot more like gritted teeth for a moment. "Oh God." He looks up at the ceiling, collecting his thoughts.

"My mother is a very sweet, very nice woman, who, like you, is a fairly recent widow. She had fifty good years in with Dad, but that doesn't make her miss him less. It makes her pretty lonely.

"I try to get up here every weekend, but Andrea befriended

her to help lighten my load back in the day, and I was stupid and supported that. Then things with Andrea went to hell and I discovered she's been using us all. My mother, though, can't quite grasp that her 'friend' isn't worth trying to repair things with."

I realize that I'm sitting there staring at him with my orange floral mug halfway to my mouth, and hastily take a sip before setting the tea aside. "I'm so sorry. Maybe if your mother was less lonely, it would hurt her less to kick this fake friend to the curb? I could help."

I know all about being that desperately lonely. In the early days of my widowhood, when I was stumbling around without direction or anyone to go to, predators started to seek me out. They were like sharks scenting blood in the water.

Some of them infiltrated my online support groups looking for victims to use for sex, attention, and cash. They circled around, spewing false sympathy and understanding, telling me they were there if I ever needed to talk. All the while, they were planning to use every single thing I told them as leverage to get what they wanted.

Unfortunately for them, I was loyal to both Manny and his child, and when they pushed too much, I got angry. Then they would see something in me that was too strong for them to bother with, and flee.

Unfortunately, that type of man has been the only kind of person to show any real interest in talking to me, outside of my three fellow widows.

I've tried to be understanding about how my friend pool suddenly dried up. Depressed people are depressing to be around. But when I lost Manny, I saw too much of the worst side of people—including people I thought I knew, and once counted as friends. How easily so many abandon others in need, or see them as wounded prey.

"You look very sad suddenly," he says in a low, musing voice, instead of answering my question.

"I can sympathize with your mom. That's all. I understand about being an isolated new widow. It does leave you vulnerable, especially if you trust the wrong people." I gaze at him wistfully.

Please don't be the wrong person for me to trust. Please don't be using me, or planning some screwed-up prank. I'm tired of feeling like we lost the last good man on Earth when Manny died.

"Andrea has a real nose for people in pain. I worry that she might try to exploit you too if you run into her before I can get her to leave." He actually sounds worried.

I can't help but smile. "I don't plan to let her ask me for any favors. And I don't know why she'd talk to me. I mean, people like her ... don't notice people like me." *So why do you?* I want to ask, but bite back the question because I don't want to offend him. He might genuinely be interested. He might genuinely be trying to be nice.

"She'll notice you soon enough if she sees that *I've* noticed you." His mouth works, and I see the disgust in his eyes and realize that he's trying to warn me.

I feel a little dubious about his whole situation all of a sudden. How broken up *are* they if she's still hanging on with both hands? Can she be as crazy as he says, or is he one of those guys who call all their exes crazy gold diggers?

We're staring at each other silently now, I realize suddenly, and hastily drain my tea to fill the silence. "So your ex just won't leave, and she's using your mother as a ticket to stay around and bother you. Maybe you should get a hotel room. That might alert your mother to the fact that there's more of a problem going on than she has let herself see."

He sits back, a little frown on his face as he mulls the idea over. "Well, the approach has its merits, but I'm wondering just how effective that would be. It would upset my mother, but would probably cause less strife than whatever Andrea will get up to. And no matter how things turn out, I will end up with some breathing room."

"That's the spirit." I give him a tiny, forced smile.

"Yes, well. I have occasional moments of brilliance, even when I'm tired from the road—and Andrea." He rubs his face, takes another big swallow from his mug, and sets it aside, looking around. "I notice that the place is rather sparse."

My cheeks start heating up again, and my gaze drops to the tops of my slippers. "Yes."

"Didn't you want a tree or some decorations? Or a gift for yourself?" He's looking at the snow bunny, wrapped in newspaper—a bright one, but still a newspaper.

He's not getting it. *Of course not, he's rich.* I let out a sad little laugh, and rub my temple. "It doesn't matter what I want for myself or my little girl for Christmas. We can't get it because there is no money."

He blinks for a moment, and I nod sadly to myself. Just from the look on his face, I know he's never had to go hungry so that someone else could eat. He's never wondered where the rent is coming from, or whether there will be money to pay for heat next week.

"I didn't realize," he says finally, and then shoots me another confused look. "Don't you have any friends that could help?"

I can't help it. I laugh. "Around here? Do you have any idea how the standard New York rich conservative treats people who have to depend on charity to survive, even if we work more than full time? I don't have any friends."

He blinks in shock. "Then ... there's no family, no husband, no friends ... no Christmas? Not at all?"

I have to squash a surge of anger. How can he be this dense? The guy really must have lived a very spoiled, privileged life if he's having that much trouble processing the reality of my life. "Just the one present for my daughter, and we are lucky to have that."

"I'm sorry, you mentioned that you work so much, and so ..." He shakes his head. "How can you work more than full time and still be struggling like this?"

Now I want to cry. But I just keep that fake smile on. "Welcome to life outside the one percent. It's not very pretty, and it's not very fair.

"I'm not lazy. I'm not unskilled. And I probably put in way more work in a week than anyone you have ever met. But this, along with the VA denying me my husband's death benefits, is what I wake up to every day."

I stare at him defiantly. I'm suddenly so angry that I don't care if he rejects me. If he does, he's not the man I had a crush on anyway. He's just another Hollywood fake, and the James I've come to have a real crush on, just another role.

I prepare myself for that, just as I once prepared myself when the two plain-clothed men from the Department of Defense showed up on my doorstep the day I was told I'd become widow. But what I see on his face instead of disdain is confusion and grief.

"I'm sorry," he murmurs in such a gentle tone that it makes my heart ache. "I've always tried to be sympathetic toward others, but I live in a certain bubble. I know that. I don't have any acquaintance with the kind of hardships that you describe, and I wish that you didn't either."

I lick my lips and look down, hearing him move over and sit on the couch beside me. Not near enough to touch, but when his weight settles on the couch with me it feels as intimate as a caress. "It wasn't supposed to be like this. Manny and I worked hard. We were young and responsible. The VA was supposed to take care of us, even if something happened to him."

I can't keep the confusion, grief, and anger of the last two years out of my voice. Knowing that our men died for our country, just for our country to turn around and forget every promise it made us ... it still stings. *The honor of soldiers still exists, but the honor of their ultimate leaders seems to be gone.*

He reaches over and puts his huge hand over mine, and I turn my head to see his blurry form leaning toward me. "I'm sorry. Again, I fully admit, I don't understand. Maybe I ... maybe I just wanted to believe that the world was a fairer place than this. But I suppose that I should know better."

The self-deprecating irony in his voice disarms me, and I wipe my eyes with my free hand, a little impatient with myself. "No, I'm sorry. I shouldn't unload all my problems on you."

"It's fine. I just unloaded some of my problems on you, after all." He leans back a little, considering me. "You know, when I ordered us turnovers in the cafe, I swear that you looked at them like the waitress had brought you a basket of gold. Even Cindy looked more excited than I'm used to seeing."

He's puzzled, not condemning. I squash a fresh surge of embarrassment. "That's because we haven't had a treat like that in a very long time."

I'm not used to people knowing just how badly off I am. "I'm not looking for any handouts or anything. I don't want your pity," I mumble.

"You don't have it," he assures me. "I would have to look down on you to pity you, and I don't."

I look up at him again, slowly, and see the warmth in his eyes. "In fact," he murmurs, moving closer as his hand squeezes mine gently, "I would say you're one of the bravest women that I have ever met."

The floor seems to tilt under me a little. I swallow, staring at him, unable to believe the tenderness in his gaze. Tears fill my eyes then, and I look away, out the undecorated window at the black street beyond.

"I know you won't ask me for help. You're not the sort, are you? Not looking for handouts at all, even when you desperately need it." He sounds a little astonished, and I sniffle and give him a wan smile.

"I've never asked anyone for more than my baby and I need," I say honestly. He's still holding my hand, the warm smoothness of his palm cradling the back of mine almost tenderly, and it sends tingles shooting up my arm. The warmth melts away my grief and my shame, as if it were a layer of ice around my heart.

"You should be asking for more. You deserve more." He's stroking the back of my hand now. My knees clench together under my nightgown. *Is this affection, or is he seducing me? Is there a difference, aside from whether his heart is in it or not?*

"Around here ... nobody likes a freeloader," I murmur—and am startled when he laughs.

"My God, you're the anti-Andrea. Lorena, dear ... please. I'm asking you, as a favor to me, let me do something for you and Cindy for Christmas." The plea in his eyes startles me into silence, and he goes on. "The job opportunity is a happy coincidence. I'm talking about a gift for you, and for your little girl."

I stare at him and draw a deep breath. I want to ask him to save us. To take us under his wing, to protect us and help us out just enough that I can get by until that damned death benefit finally comes through.

But he's talking about a Christmas gift, not a long commitment. My brows draw together as I try to let my mind venture out from "what we need most desperately" territory to "what it would be fun to have" for the first time in years. It takes me a minute.

"Coats," I manage finally. "Heavy down coats. Something

that's actually warm enough for me and for Cindy. Hers in pink. It's her favorite."

He blinks in surprise, and then offers a faint, wistful smile. "That's ... not much of a gift."

"Have you ever been out in a New York winter for a long time without a proper coat? I walk dogs as part of my living. Trust me, it's a great gift." But then my tentative smile fades as uncertainty fills me. "I don't have anything to give you in return, though."

"Well, that's not entirely true," he replies in a tone so smooth it sends a shiver through me. His eyes hood slightly. "Though to be completely honest, what I want for Christmas from you is not something I can expect as a gift from anyone who feels obliged to give it. It's only given by someone who wants to receive it back."

He's moved closer to me and our knees are almost brushing now. I swallow, amazed that this is happening, amazed at myself for wanting it to happen.

My hand is on his shoulder; I don't know how it got there. I can feel the warm curve of muscle under my hands, beneath a thin chocolate-colored turtleneck that's nothing like the giant sweater from earlier. It clings and shifts, sliding like silk across my fingers and molding to every contour of his rippling abs.

The sight distracts me until I feel his breath on my face and look up to see his mouth inches from mine. My eyes slide closed as I tremble. *This is happening. It's really, really happening.*

When he kisses me, something detonates inside of me, and my fingers dig into his back through his shirt. Our bodies press together as he crouches over me on the couch. His mouth is hot and firm, his touch decisive as he takes me into his arms.

My head fills with a warm haze, and I kiss him back a little clumsily, my whole body feeling ready to melt into him. He lets out a contented little grunt and intensifies the kiss, his hands starting to slide over my back. *Oh, that's it. Don't stop. Don't stop.*

We keeping kissing and stroking each other and I suddenly don't know where this is going. I'm losing track of how long we've been in each other arms. My body aches with the need for more, in a way I just haven't felt before. Not even with Manny.

Sex with Manny was about tenderness, and giving, and very slowly learning each other. Manny never hurt me, but he never learned to satisfy me either. We were too young, too new at sex, too shy, and he didn't know how to ask—and neither did I.

With one kiss, James has already sent me to another level. My head swims. My heart pounds, and for a long time, all I can feel are the silken caresses of hands and lips on me. The faint buzzing somewhere off in the background is a mere nuisance, like the hum of a fly.

But then, before we can move on toward anything further, James reluctantly stops, and I feel him sigh through his nose against my cheek. He breaks the kiss and draws back gently, and I look up at him in hazy-eyed confusion. "Phone," he mutters apologetically. "Only family has this number."

Damn, I think, but I don't speak it aloud. Family needs are family needs, even if I'm an inch from dragging him up to bed.

He leaves me shivering and tingling all over as he checks the phone screen and then answers it. "Mom? What are you doing up so late?"

My heart sinks. Even before the concern in his eyes ignites into anger, I know. I might have a lot of baggage of my own ... but it's his baggage that's pushing us apart right now.

"Look, I went out for a drink because Andrea kept trying to get into my room." He listens, and huffs a sigh. "Oh, she did, did she? Good thing I'm not in town yet. I'll be back soon."

I watch him lie to his mother to hide where he really is, and feel a weird mix of guilt and worry. But if his mother's reporting everything back to Andrea because she mistakenly trusts her, then it's at least a little understandable. I still watch and listen, wary of any little warning sign that I might be offering my trust to the wrong man.

He hangs up and shoots me that same apologetic look, with a hint of the same frustration I feel. "I'm so sorry. The last thing I want to do is kiss and run, but Andrea's out literally searching the streets for my car, and I don't want her finding it parked in front of your place. The last thing you need is her on your back."

"No, I don't need that at all." Maybe I don't need any of this drama. My body might ache from the sudden withdrawal of his touch, but if the price is harassment, I'm not sure I can take much of it. "Thank you. I ... will you call me?"

My voice sounds almost pitifully sad, and the guilt on his face deepens. "You said coats. You'll have them. And a surprise, as well. I promise."

I blink at him. "What ... kind of surprise?"

He winks. "You'll see."

He kisses me a last time before he walks out, leaving me watching him breathlessly through the front window as he walks away. My lips still tingle, and my head's full of confusion now. *Should I be happy? Or should I be running in the other direction?*

CHAPTER 6

James

I'm absolutely ready to strangle Andrea with my bare hands for getting in the way of the sweetest kiss I've ever tasted. So I know I can't go straight home. She'll be there, and if I see her before I cool off there's going to be a confrontation, and my poor mother will end up in tears.

AT LEAST MOM knows I'm all right and doing something normal. I often go down to the one late night bar in Phoenicia for a few pints and maybe a hot brandy when it's cold enough. In good weather, I can just walk down the hill.

BUT THIS TIME, it's snowing thinly again, and there's a threat of a snowstorm coming through just in time for Christmas. With all the mess going on with Andrea, I know that Mom's anxiety is through the roof, so I guess I shouldn't be surprised that she called, even without Andrea bugging her.

I absolutely have to make sure that if Andrea finds me, it's nowhere near Lorena's, so I head out to the bar as quickly as I can. Fifteen minutes later I'm sliding onto a stool at the shiplap and carved wood bar of the one late night watering hole in town.

THE PLACE SMELLS of woodsmoke from the potbelly stove, and the heater is rumbling away as well, keeping things cozy despite it being in the twenties outside. A few men sit at the bar, barely glancing up as I come in. Despite having family here, I'm an out-of-towner, and get treated as such by most.

I'M NOT the only out-of-towner in here tonight, though. A couple in their early thirties sits in the corner in high-end down coats like the ones Lorena wants—but in drab colors, the woman in olive green and the man in navy. Her red braid glimmers like copper in the semi-dark. He holds a beer he doesn't drink in one long-fingered hand and looks back at her with occasional sad-puppy eyes when he thinks she isn't looking.

COUPLE TROUBLES. They seem universal sometimes, though they vary in circumstances. I look away politely as the burly, Navy-tattooed bartender comes up to take my order.

I ORDER MY HOT BRANDY—a toddy this time, with honey and lemon. The bartender throws a gob of honey the size of a golf ball in the bottom, and I suddenly remember how carefully Lorena handled her last tiny bit of honey while serving tea. I wish I hadn't been forced from her side tonight. I wanted to show her that despite the brief amount of time we've known each other that I'm already very interested in her—and in making her life better.

I DISTRACT myself by looking around more—and am startled when I realize I've overlooked a nearby familiar face: Dr. Whitman's. He's perched two stools down from my seat and looks over at me with his small eyes twinkling, a smile hidden somewhere in his beard. "Trouble at home?" he rumbles, his booming voice a perfect fit for his Saint Nick looks.

"TROUBLE CAME TO MY HOME. My family's great." I turn to him and offer a hand. "Merry Christmas, Dr. Whitman. How are you and your son?"

HE LETS out a laugh that he cuts off quickly, as if aware that his voice is big and there are men with alcohol-induced headaches squinting in the shadows of this place. "Well, quite well. It's Jack's favorite time of year, of course. I'm sure he'll be hitting the slopes as soon as his holiday duties are finished."

"HOLIDAY DUTIES?" The Whitmans are more than eccentric; sometimes they can be downright cryptic.

"OH, nothing serious. Decorations, arrangements, meetings with family. All the things you'd probably expect." He smiles broadly and scoops up his small glass of schnapps, savoring a small sip. "My son's flighty, but responsible when it matters."

HE LOOKS over at the couple in the corner, who appear to be surreptitiously watching us. "Friends of yours?" I ask quietly.

HE CHUCKLES and shakes his head. "No, nothing like that at all. I seem to have attracted some curiosity-seekers again."

"HUH." I look back at the pair. They certainly interact with each other like a couple. "I just thought they were out on a date."

"WELL THEY SHOULD BE ON A DATE," he grumbles good-naturedly. "There's not enough romance in this world any more. Even with mistletoe everywhere, some pairs just refuse to smooch. It's a damn shame."

I THINK WISTFULLY of that lingering kiss with Lorena and nod. "I think you're absolutely right."

WE TALK and drink for a little while, and I'm two toddies in and starting to relax before Andrea finds us. We've been talking about my indecision over what to get Lorena on such short notice, trying to sort out what I can get her that will really impress her. Dr. Whitman is good at making me laugh, and better at finishing his drinks. He loves his schnapps.

. . .

I'M SMILING in the middle of a joke when the door bangs open and Andrea stalks in, bundled in silver fox fur, scowling like an angry mother who has just caught her misbehaving son. She sweeps her glaring gaze around like a spotlight as she stands in the doorway until the bartender yells, "Close the fucking door!" She squeaks in outrage and stumbles inside.

I SIGH and drop my face into my hand, and Whitman chuckles and pats me on the shoulder with a meaty palm. Then Andrea sees me, and I hear her stiletto heels clack across the floor toward me so loudly that a couple of the drunks grunt in pain. "Where the hell have you been?"

"GETTING AWAY FROM YOU, you crazy shrew." I keep my voice low, but I'm done pretending that I'm all right with her ridiculous behavior. "Why haven't you left yet?"

SHE STARES AT ME, fists on hips, while a few of the others chuckle at her expression. "You should go home," she snaps. "Your mother is worried."

I ROLL MY EYES. "My mother picked up a phone and talked to me herself. She's fine, and she knows that I am fine. And at this point, she also knows more than a little of what you have been up to."

I CAN FEEL myself being watched, probably by Whitman, while I confront Andrea as calmly as I can. Inside, I'm wrestling down the kind of rage that will make a man drink too much, drive too fast, and fuck too hard. I have to dial it back.

"There's someone else, isn't there," she demands. I feel my heart skip a beat. It's ridiculous to let her nosiness worry me, but just as with my mother, I feel like I have to protect Lorena from the worst side of Andrea's personality.

"I don't see how anything in my life is your business anymore," I reply in a low, hard voice. "And I don't understand why you continue to follow me around, pestering me. I can't even go out and have a drink without your showing up to bother me."

I notice her glancing around, as if she's realizing for the first time that she's throwing a hissy fit in public. A few bar patrons have phones out and are recording her. "You should still come home now," she says, much more uncertainly.

"Think I'm going to finish my drink first," I tell her coldly.

She looks around at everyone watching us, her mouth working, and then looks back at me. "You are being difficult for no reason."

"Look, Andrea, it's pretty clear now that either you're hitting the cocaine and tequila an awful lot, or you've lost your damn mind. We broke up over half a year ago. And as of tomorrow, either you leave, or I'll be staying at a hotel instead of my own mother's home, just to get away from you."

HER EYES WIDEN. I've just admitted in front of cameras that we're quits. It's something we had both been avoiding—her out of pride, and me because I wanted a break from dating and didn't want every other woman like her beating down my door.

"I CAN'T BELIEVE YOU," she murmurs, astounded, and I let out a harsh laugh.

"Oh, I imagine that you can't. That part of your mind doesn't seem to be working right now. Just know that if you kick up a tantrum on your way out tomorrow and upset my mother, I really *will* get a restraining order against you—and I'll go straight to the press about doing so."

HER JAW DROPS AS if I just slapped her. She knows I have her dead to rights. If her diva reputation gets too enormous, she won't even manage to get a job as a trophy wife. She'll be kicked off the rich-guy dating market just as she's been kicked off of modeling agencies' client lists.

WITHOUT ANOTHER WORD, she turns on her heel and stalks out, slamming the door hard behind her.

THANK GOD. "SORRY GUYS," I call out, and hear a few grumbles and more than a few sympathetic chuckles. I turn to the bartender and order a round for the bar, and the grumbling stops.

Dr. Whitman clears his throat, and I turn back to his merry face as he lifts his glass. "Nicely done. I imagine she'll try some parting shot or another, but I believe you took the wind from her sails when you mentioned going public."

I smirk and reach for my glass. The toddy's already cooling. "Well, I'd rather be spending my evening with the young mother I told you about."

"Of course you would!" He drains his schnapps and calls out for his free one. "She sounds lovely. And by the way, I think I know how you might make her Christmas just a little bit brighter, since that's of concern to you. You said that you wanted to surprise her? I've thought of the perfect thing, and I may be of help."

A weight lifts off of me, and I lift an eyebrow at him. "What did you have in mind?"

CHAPTER 7

Lorena

"Mommy, Mommy! Wake up!" comes the cry, piercing through muddled dreams of James's kisses. I flail awake, eyes flying open to a room full of pale, snow-reflected sunlight.

"Unh," I manage, and then shake off the cobwebs and look up at the pink-robed sprite bouncing at the side of my bed. She's not scared; she's *excited*. "What's this about, sweetie? Did it snow again?"

"No, not yet! Come see the yard!" She grabs me by the hand, and for a moment I fear she's going to try and drag me out of bed. But then she smiles and backs off. "Come on!"

. . .

I CHECK MY WATCH. Seven thirty. The light trickling in my window still has a faint tinge of peach-pink to it: dawn light. *Ugh, it's not even Christmas yet*, I think as I sit up and rub my eyes. "All right, all right, just give me a minute."

Whatever it is, she can barely wait long enough for me to put my hair back in a ponytail and throw on my robe and slippers. Now and again as she waits for me she runs back down the hall to a window facing the front of the house. Then she runs back to me, beaming because of whatever she's seeing outside.

I DIDN'T SLEEP WELL. James left me hot and bothered, and a little ashamed of it. It feels like I'm doing something wrong by wanting someone other than Manny. But my heart seems to have already decided.

I WANT to be back in his arms. I want to feel his kiss again. Remembering the way he cupped my breast through the flannel of my nightgown makes me shiver and gasp and wish he were here again.

I SHOULDN'T BE LETTING myself get distracted by this. Whatever has Cindy bouncing off the walls could be completely benign, or she could be misinterpreting something dangerous. Hastily, I walk after her down the hall, tying my robe around me as I go.

I LOOK OUT THE WINDOW ... and do an immediate double take. For a moment, it genuinely looks like I am looking down at someone else's front lawn.

. . .

The pair of flowering dogwoods that flank the front gate, the little spruce we cover with squirrel food, the old wrought-iron fence surrounding the property, the mailbox, the lamp ... all of them are covered in garlands of fir branches, holly, mistletoe, and poinsettias. Several strings of solar lights wind through the decorations, still offering faint gold and white gleams.

I stare so long that my eyes start hurting, and then reach down and pinch myself through the sleeve of my robe. I'm definitely not dreaming. "What in the world?" I mumble breathlessly.

Once we're both wrapped in coats and have proper shoes on, we go out onto the porch to look around at the unexpected decorations. The trees are trimmed. The squirrels are clustered around a new feeder, already filled, that has been fastened to the tree just across from my kitchen window.

Aluminum-framed deer with contours formed from strands of lights bob their heads in the grass, like they are grazing. A small generator rumbles away in a corner of the yard, keeping them going. There's a stack of gas cans next to it, under a snow-spattered tarp that has blown aside partway to expose them.

Someone has even built a snowman. It is chunky and unrefined, clearly the work of someone who hasn't built one in years. I can see the prints of huge gloved hands where the man who made it struggled with getting the head round and the carrot nose even.

. . .

"Who did this, Mommy? Was it Santa Claus?"

I know who it is right away. James mentioned a surprise. He's wealthy, he likes me ... *he kissed me*. He could pull this off, especially with a little help. And he actually has some reason to—at least if he's not pulling off an elaborate hoax.

"No, Santa's too busy at this time of year. But he does have some friends that help him out. I guess we'll have to see who shows up to take credit." I wink at her, and she giggles and wanders out across the yard to look at everything.

I haven't had a man try to impress me in years. And this ... brings quiet tears to my eyes as I watch my daughter toddle around happily in her own little wonderland. "It's so beautiful," I murmur.

I catch sight of someone watching us from across the street, and turn with a smile, expecting it to be James. My smile fades immediately, and I feel my delight in the moment deflate slightly as I see who is standing there.

Andrea Case stands beside a cute gold Porsche, wrapped in furs, with gold-rimmed sunglasses hiding her eyes. Her arms are folded, and her mouth is a line. I'd probably have recognized her from her attitude alone if I didn't already know what she looked like. I know at once that she knows who did this as well —and that her presence here is a declaration of war.

. . .

She starts walking slowly across the street toward me. She would look more menacing if she wasn't wobbling on stiletto heels on a just-plowed street, but I still don't want Cindy to have to deal with whatever crap is about to come out of her mouth. I call out to my daughter to get her attention.

"Sweetie, if you want to keep playing in the snow, I need you to go put your scarf on." Cindy has a favorite purple scarf that she got from the church last year, and I know mention of it will tear her away from the surprise. It will also take her a little digging to find.

Her face lights up and she nods, turning to amble inside. I help her up the steep front steps and she wanders over to the coat closet. I close the door behind her—and only then turn to face the woman glaring at me from just outside my gate.

"May I help you?" I say calmly as I walk down the stairs.

"Who are you?" she demands. "I just saw James drive away from here not half an hour ago. What interest does he have in you? Answer me!"

My heart starts pounding. I've endured a lot of scorn from rich city bitches like this one, who come up for weekend vacations with their big egos and nasty opinions. I've learned to keep the pain and humiliation deep in my aching chest, and wear a mask of polite indifference, like retail workers use. "If you're talking about Mr. Norris," I say in such an even tone that it startles her, "I'm being hired as his mother's driver and assistant."

SHE WILTS SLIGHTLY, her aggression melting enough that I can see the confusion behind it. "Then why would he do all of this?" She waves her hand around. "I saw him leave with that ... overdressed mall Santa he was drinking with." Her hand settles on the gate latch, as if she's about to invite herself in.

I FOLD my arms across my chest as I come to stand firm on the other side of the gate. She's got almost a foot of height on me and is obviously nasty and possibly violent. But if she thinks she's stepping one foot closer to my home and my baby daughter, she's out of her mind.

"HE WOULD DO all of this because the man's trying to get me to take on a high-needs client on short notice during the holidays, and he wants to make sure I'm willing to drop everything and help him out. Besides, I have a two year old. Without his help, she wouldn't have much of a Christmas at all."

I LOOK her right in the eyes as I say this, and I do not look away. I feel sick inside, but she's not rational and I can't let her take control of this situation. *I wish James was here to sort this out.*

. . .

"Wait. You're the new assistant he's hiring for his mom?" Again, there's more confusion in her voice than relief. "But you're just the help. Why be nice to you at all? Clearly you need the money too much to turn down the job, regardless of the time of year." She runs her hand over the aging iron of the gate and scoffs.

It's like a kick in the stomach, but it only fuels my anger—and my resolve. "Because unlike most of you spoiled children who call yourselves elite, he actually gives a damn about people who aren't doing as well as he is."

She just scoffs again, her eyes widening, as if she's astounded that I would be this stupid. "What do you even know about him? I can't believe that even a Cinderella-wannabe like you would be this stupid!"

This time, the blow doesn't fuel my anger—it smothers it as she talks. The cold starts to trickle in to replace it. Cold, hard reality that I've been trying to ignore since the moment James sat down at a small café table with me and Cindy. "I'm sorry, but I don't know what you're talking about."

"Well of course you don't. He's picked the most naive, desperate piece of ass he could find in this shithole town."

My eyes narrow. "I think you're the one misreading the situation between myself and Mr. Norris." Inside, it feels like icy fingernails are digging at my heart. "All I am expecting out of Mr. Norris and his mother is a steady job."

"AND DO you think that your work for his mother is all *he's* expecting?" she snaps back, though with a bit less force. "I don't think he picked you because you're particularly qualified."

I LIFT MY CHIN. "Actually I'm a certified nursing assistant with years of experience as an attendant and driver." *Was a CNA, anyway.* I had just gotten my license when Manny died, and the need to care for Cindy has made it impossible for me to commute for a real job. But it is still true, and I brandish it like a weapon as I continue to glare at Andrea.

"OH," she mumbles, suddenly looking slightly embarrassed. Then she takes a deep breath before speaking again with something almost like sympathy in her voice. "Well ... look. Just keep in mind that he's the kind of man who will toy with the help if she's pretty enough and he's bored. I've known him for a long time, and I know how easy it is for him to break hearts— whether he means it or not."

THE HELP. With those words, reality crashes back in on me, and I feel my heart sink into my boots. *Of course.*

ANDREA MIGHT BE A RAGING bitch with ulterior motives, and I'm not falling for this pseudo-caring persona she's trying on me right now, but she does have a point. Sure, James might be genuinely attracted to me, but this whole time I haven't understood why he's been acting so nice to me. I can't help but second-guess James in that moment. *Is that all I am? Just some nobody that he can screw for fun?*

I wish I could dismiss it, just to spite this woman who is standing here expecting me to crumble. But I have years of experience with New York classism. I can't expect a Cinderella story; I can't actually expect that James will save me from loneliness and poverty. All I can expect is a good job, and maybe a flattering bit of flirting.

His kiss last night confused the reality at hand and stoked my crush to a fever pitch. But it doesn't mean he loves me. He barely knows me. He may well just want sex from someone who isn't a complete ass.

And that's all right, if he's honest about it—as much as it might hurt me to give in, knowing that a little bit of sex is not all that I want from him. But ... I have to protect myself, whether my physical relationship with James goes any further or not. And this woman's reminder may be brutal, but it's also ... timely.

"They are hiring me for my skills," I reply firmly, feeling like I've swallowed poison. "That is all that they are going to get."

. . .

SHE TURNS AND STALKS AWAY, a look of satisfaction on her face. "Good."

I WANT to cry as I watch her leave. But instead, I lift my chin, put my smile back on, and walk back up my steps to take my daughter out to play in the yard.

CHAPTER 8

Lorena

I get the job. It isn't that much of a surprise, but I have to hide the relief that rushes through me when James's mother hands me my advance. I hold myself stiffly and professionally the whole time, leaving James in apparent confusion as he walks me back to my car.

"Is something wrong?" he asks as we walk down the broad driveway of his mother's twenty-room Victorian. I had not wanted to ruin my chances by rudely parking my beater in their driveway.

I look around at the decorations in her yard, noting how much they resemble my own, and feel my emotions wrestle inside of me again. This crush is screwing with my ability to be objective. "No, I'm happy," I say, still not letting myself draw too near him, nor responding to the little brushes of his hand against mine. "This job helps us a lot. Cindy loved the yard decorations, and your mom likes me."

Also, Andrea is conspicuously gone. Her cute little car is

missing from the driveway. She must have come to give me her little "talk" on her way out of town.

A parting shot. It makes me a little suspicious, both of what she said and of Andrea's motives. Yes, I've pretty much come to expect every rich person to be classist and shallow, but at the same time, I sat there and watched James struggle to grow beyond that—for my sake—after having barely met me.

Would he really make himself vulnerable and show himself to be less than perfect, if it was all an act to get me into bed? I don't know. But I'm now glad I haven't been colder to him—even if I'm backing off for my own protection.

"Okay. You just seem ... closed off." The confusion in his voice hurts my heart.

I give him a sad smile. It's too bad, really, that there can't be more between us than a friendship and maybe some light flirtation. But I have to be careful. It won't just be me who gets hurt if I let some rich guy screw up my life.

He doesn't need to know that I want him so badly that I cried in the bathroom before driving over for the interview. Or that I cleaned myself up right after, put my face on, and soldiered on. For my baby's sake, if not for the sake of my pride.

"It's because I kissed you, isn't it?" he ventures as we turn the corner onto the street.

"It left me ... confused," I hedge as I walk up to my car, which is so covered after two hours that I can't see its dull brown color. I pull out my scraper and brush a thick crush of snow off the windshield. The flakes are still coming, blowing in sheets across the road.

"Should I apologize? I really don't want to, since it was great. But if it made you uncomfortable—"

"James," I say firmly as I work on my car. "I liked it. If I did not, I wouldn't have gone along with it. But I don't know you, and I have to be careful."

He seems a little shocked, as if it never occurred to him that a woman who was attracted to him would back off for any reason. But instead of arguing, he says simply, "How do I earn your trust, then?"

I bite my lip. He seems so sincere. If only he wasn't a brilliant actor. I can't be sure if he's acting now. "Just don't lie to me. I'll sort out whether I can trust you as more than a friend if you do that for me."

He spreads his hands as he leans against the side of my car. "I'm an open book," he says as snowflakes fall into his bronze-colored hair. "What do you want to know?"

"Everything," I say breathlessly, since it's the most honest answer I can give. I do want to know everything—I want to know his favorite breakfast, and whether he talks in his sleep. I want to know what his weight feels like against me in the dark.

But right now, I just want to get to know him well enough to know whether he can be trusted—with me and in Cindy's presence too.

He relaxes slightly, and flashes that Hollywood smile again. "It's the same on my end. I want to know everything about you."

I close my eyes, his smile threatening to melt the careful boundary I'm trying to put up. *Andrea didn't have my best interests in mind. But it still doesn't mean she wasn't telling the truth. Only time will tell.*

"Let's try tea again, then. Tomorrow night, if you're free." With the advance his mother insisted on giving me, I'm going to buy a box of tea and a jar of real honey, and I'll be taking Cindy into town for cocoa on my own money.

"After dinner? I still need to bring your gift." He looks hopeful. Too hopeful. I remind myself to be cautious.

He sees my face and grows more serious. "I'm willing to do what it takes to show you I'm sincere, Lorena."

I can't help the warmth in my smile when he says that. "We'll see."

It doesn't fully dawn on me that Cindy and I are going to be able to have a real dinner tonight until I go through my wallet as I sit in my car. The bundle of twenties is much thicker than I thought. But mixed with the shock and elation is another set of drawbacks, just like my having to be cautious with James.

It embarrasses me a little, and makes me just a touch worried that James's mother, Janet, will only disappoint me later. But I try to reassure myself. *She's wealthy, and lonely, and she likes me.* And I can already tell that even if James turns out to be flighty, his mother won't be cruel.

It's Christmas Eve and it seems like everyone's in the grocery store, bustling over the things they forgot for tonight's dinner. Cindy sits in the cart seat as I push it around, forcing myself to take my time and focus on ingredients and things that will keep.

"Are we having pizza for Christmas?" Cindy looks a little worried that she'll miss out on cheesy goodness as she watches me bundle a whole frozen chicken into the cart.

"We'll order pizza tonight, and I'll roast a chicken tomorrow." And stuff it, and have enough for leftovers for a couple of days before I make soup. My mouth waters just at the thought.

"Yay, pizza early!" Cindy is easy to please. And so, I realize as I fill my cart, am I.

Milk, eggs, string cheese, butter, fresh fruit, mushrooms. Frozen veggies and meats. Canned goods. Baking supplies. My spice rack needs replenishing. So does my sugar jar. So does everything. And now I can actually do that.

I've learned to shop smart and stretch everything, and it pays off now as I need only a quarter of the cash I was given to cover the grocery bill. I feel a little giddy at the thought. Nobody who hasn't lined up at church with an empty stomach fully understands the sheer joy of the thought *I can afford to buy my own food.*

My only other splurge, besides the raw honey, happens when I stop in at a shoe store right before they close. I buy us both warm waterproof boots with new, anti-slip soles, and as tall as our knees. They don't have pink, so Cindy gets purple.

On the way home, she sings in the car to take the place of the broken radio, and I smile and think of James. I still wish he was here with us. I comfort myself knowing that at least we'll have another tentative chance, and that he's made sure that he and his family can have a peaceful Christmas together.

Andrea. She knew exactly what she was doing when she reminded me of James and I being from two different worlds.

She never once even tried to claim that she was anything but a heartless opportunist. She simply acted like what she was doing was normal for all her kind, and like I was a fool for thinking otherwise. *And maybe I am.*

But it still warms my heart to dream that James is different.

I can't stop thinking about it all through my quiet Christmas in with Cindy. On Christmas day she and her snow bunny Percy and her new boots go on adventures around the yard while I watch, and sometimes help out. Inside, the chicken is roasting, and an apple pie I made from scratch is cooling on the table.

But what I'm really looking forward to is what I've got planned after dinner—my date with James. I know that's dangerous, but my heart doesn't care.

We have to go in before the chicken is ready, because the sky has gone the color of steel and the few flakes drifting down from it are starting to fall thicker. The coming storm leaves me wrestling with my fears: a blackout, loss of heat, the job falling through somehow, James not showing up. My ambivalence only makes things worse.

My stomach jumps around all through dinner, until finally even Cindy can tell something's wrong. "Does your tummy hurt, Mommy?" she asks with worry in her tone as I cut her chicken into small bites for her.

"No, my heart hurts," I say honestly. "Lots of good things are happening, like James getting me a job with his mom. But Mommy's worried that they might not last." *That James isn't who he says he is. That he's using me, and doesn't care about me at all.*

"You should just be happy while things are happy, Mommy." She shoves a cube of chicken into her mouth and chews enthusiastically. "I like James. Is he bringing us coats?"

"Yes, later tonight," I murmur, and hope my daughter's right about him.

Cindy has worn herself out in the cold, and as soon as the sugar from the pie wears off she falls asleep on the couch and I carry her to bed. Once she's changed and settled in I go back down and sit waiting, pretending to read one of my library books.

The wind rises to a whine in the eaves and I look outside through the slats in my bent and aging blinds at a street now only half-visible behind swirling curtains of flakes. *Maybe he won't come after all. Maybe it's inconvenient to drive in this mess. Maybe it isn't even safe.*

Twenty minutes and a single page of my novel later, I hear a car door slam outside. My heart leaps and I turn around to peer out at the front walk. A tall figure with a bundle in his arms is coming in the gate, shoulders hunched against the pelting flakes.

I run to the door and open it for him before he can knock. He stands there for a moment, surprised, two floppy presents wrapped in bright paper hanging from his arms. "Hi!" he manages after a moment.

"You made it," I breathe, my emotions at war inside of me. I let him pass and he looks around as I shut the door behind him.

"I wouldn't miss it," he replies, and flashes a million-dollar grin when he catches me blushing.

CHAPTER 9

Lorena

Cindy's out for the night. James and I drink my new tea and chat about everything; his mother, Andrea's huffy departure, and about how each of our Christmases went with our families. It's warm and easy, the only awkwardness coming from the deepening longing inside of me as we spend time together.

I still want him so badly I can barely think around it.

Finally he asks the question I wish he wouldn't. "Lorena ... did Andrea find you and say anything to you? She was trying to discourage my mother from hiring you while she was packing to go."

I set my mug down a little too hard in disgust. "Of course," I say finally. I didn't want to talk about this, but I know it needs to be brought up.

"You know she's terrible, right?" His eyes widen slightly. "Did she threaten you into backing off?"

I actually have to think about that. "Well, I didn't feel safe around her. But it's more that she brought up worries that I already had."

He rubs his face, setting his own mug down. "I was afraid of that. What did she say?"

I don't want to go into every ugly detail of it. "She told me that you would use me."

His face reddens and then pales, and he glares down at his hands before covering his eyes with them. "People planning to use you don't go to these lengths," he says in an almost pleading tone, gazing directly into my eyes once more.

"Andrea does," I remind him, and he sighs.

"Well, yes, but she's obsessed. Why do you think she couldn't move on without trying to ruin things for me with the woman I'm interested in?" He stares down at his hands again, looking sick—sick and angry. I want to hug him but I can't.

"If I really believed her, James, I wouldn't let you into my house." My low, pointed tone cuts though the tension between us and he lifts his head to look into my eyes. "I've had a crush on you for almost half my life. But somehow I'm supposed to set that aside, and take it slow, and protect myself and my little girl from being hurt."

"I don't want to hurt either of you," he says softly. He reaches over and brushes a curl of hair off my face. His fingertips leave tingling trails against my skin.

I draw a huge breath. *Tell him to go.* But my nipples are already tightening under my blouse, and I can feel my body relaxing as his hand drifts to my shoulder. "I want to believe you."

He stares at me with something like desperation in his eyes, and then ... draws his hand back. "I should go," he says hoarsely. "If I stay, I'm going to kiss you, and if I do, we may both regret it."

I take a deep breath and nod, standing with him to see him to the door. Drawing closer to him only intensifies the heat between us, and I pause, trembling. I don't want him to go. My yearning for his presence feels like a physical need, essential, like my need for air.

He won't be interested in anything beyond sex. It's too soon to expect anything else.

But there's another part of me, hungry and neglected, that has craved him for years—has craved any kind of touch—and whispers back, *would that be so bad?*

"Let's see what it's like outside," James mutters in a cautious tone. He pulls aside the blue window quilt on one of the hallway windows—and blinks. "What the hell?"

"What is it?" I ask as he brushes past me and goes for the door. I follow him—and when he unlatches it and pulls it open, a blast of wind shakes the house and throws the door wide.

Snow swirls into my home in roiling clouds and I stagger back, gasping. James wraps an arm around me to steady me and forces the door closed against the onslaught with one hard shove. The door bangs shut, and he hastily latches it. "Ugh, that was stupid of me."

In the quiet afterward, I can barely hear us panting beyond the ringing in my ears. "What's ... going on out there?"

"The storm's turned into a total whiteout. I can't drive in that." He turns his heated gaze back to me, and there's a faint note of desperation in his voice.

We stand there craving each other, and I murmur, "You'll have to stay, then." The rush of tingles through my body at the thought tells me that I'm in dangerous territory. Having him stay is too tempting.

"I'll ... sleep down here on the couch," he offers breathlessly. We're standing too close together. His arm is still around me.

"It's probably a good idea." I turn inside of his arm so I'm facing him. I feel a long shudder move through him, and see the way his eyes hood and smolder. "I can't afford to make a mistake."

"What if you're not making one?" he whispers against my lips.

The wind shakes the house again; I stiffen, and then hear a frightened cry from upstairs. "Mommy!"

James lets me go at once and I turn and bound up the stairs, back on mom duty, trying to ignore him walking up behind me. If Cindy is too upset, I'll send him off back downstairs.

I walk through her door to the side of her small bed and see her balled up under the blanket, eyes wide as they peek out from behind its edge.

"What's going on?" Cindy whimpers.

"It's okay, sweetie," I murmur as I go to sit on the edge of her bed. I wrap an arm around her. "It's just a bad snowstorm. It can't hurt us if we stay inside."

"It woke me up," she grumbles, relaxing against me. I stroke her hair, and she shivers, flinching at every rush of wind. But I stay calm, and eventually she picks up on that and relaxes. "It can't hurt us?"

"It might cause a blackout, and then it will be cold. But we've got lots of blankets, and James will help us get a generator going if we need power." I kiss the top of her head, and her mouth opens in a huge yawn.

"James is here?" she asks sleepily.

"Yes, he's here right now. He brought our coats."

"Good," she murmurs. "You should make him stay. You smile more when he's here, Mommy."

I blink down at her. *This kid.* "I'll ... think about it." Then I tuck her in and go back out in the hall to where James is waiting.

"Is she all right?" he asks gently as I emerge, and I nod, shutting the door and then moving closer to him. The door to my bedroom is right down the hall.

"She'll be fine. She's just never been in a snowstorm this strong." The wind shakes the house again and the lights flicker, but my daughter doesn't make a sound this time. She trusts me when I say she's safe.

Do I trust him, when he says that I am safe? Can I afford to?

I move up to him and brush my hands down the outsides of his arms. It's reckless, and it could get me hurt. But he's stuck here now, and I suddenly can't avoid the situation.

He moves up close to me again, and this time it feels unavoidable when we press together and he lifts me in his arms. His kiss has an edge of desperation to it that I match; he pushes me up firmly against the wall beside my bedroom door and works a thigh between my legs as his kisses intensify.

Deep down, I struggle with guilt as I remember my decision to take things slow. But when I feel him trembling against me like he's almost too excited to restrain himself, the burning heat he stokes inside of me crowds out everything else.

The wind rises to a roar again outside, covering our small sounds of pleasure as we feast on each other. Finally the kiss breaks, and he leans back, looking down at me with his chest heaving.

"Are you all right with this?" he rasps with the last of his self-control. His heart is pounding against my breasts and I can feel his erection pressing into my belly.

"You just asked me a question that I can't answer," I murmur against his lips. "If I hide from the answer ... I'll be hurting myself anyway."

What if I'm not making a mistake? What if not taking the risk ... is the mistake?

His grip tightens on me and he kisses me again, a small, feral sound escaping his throat. We kiss each other's lips until they're sore, and when he sets me on my feet I take his hand and lead him into my darkened bedroom.

I don't know what decides it for me: James's promise not to hurt us, the proof of that in his actions, Cindy wanting him to stay too, or the growing desire to spite Andrea. But even as my mixed feelings leave me shivering, I know that whatever reason I want to hang it on, this is where I wanted things to lead.

The room is small and a little drafty; I had to make window quilts from old blankets, and even with them and the plastic I shiver a little as we walk in. The iron bed is a pale shape in the dark. He nudges me toward it, kissing, nibbling, caressing the whole time, gentle and delicate but never letting up.

My bottom strikes the high edge of the mattress and he presses against me, scooting me up onto it with his hands on the small of my back. One of my flats falls off with a thump. I don't even look; I'm too wrapped up in the feel of his mouth on mine.

His hands slide my cardigan off my shoulders and toss it aside onto the bedside chair. His mouth slides down to my neck, kissing and nibbling, his teeth just brushing my flesh until I moan softly and he starts to suck.

Manny was always just as nervous as I was when going to bed. Part of it was that we were both virgins when we met, and didn't actually have that much time between deployments to sort out things like sex. But James has two decades on my late husband, and apparently, he's learned a lot from them.

He doesn't hesitate. He explores. I tremble under his hands as he slides his fingertips over every part of me, first through my dress and then up under it, caressing my thighs through my stockings. I can feel his cock pressing against me through his pants, rubbing against my bottom as I run my feet over the backs of his thighs.

I know he's marking my neck with his mouth and I submit to it, sobbing for air, the unfamiliar pleasure making me dizzy. I want to feel this good always, and forget everything.

I hear him grunt with pleasure against my neck and feel him

move lower, unfastening my dress buttons as he goes and kissing a trail down to the top of my breast. He nibbles at the soft curve of skin just above my bra, and then covers it with kisses.

He's teasing me. He pushes a little, moves his hands up and down the outsides of my thighs through my stockings, then up to the bare skin just above their garters. The brush of his big, warm hands against my chilled skin makes me cling to him, and I impatiently start sliding my own dress off my shoulders.

I help him tug the dress down to my waist and push off the bed so he can get it over my hips and away. The demure slip under it is one of the few nice ones I have, and as he starts caressing my breasts and back through the silky fabric, I'm doubly glad I wore it.

The wind keeps shaking the house and the scouring whiteness outside sends a hiss through the room. He peels off his turtleneck and tosses it aside.

I run my hands up his sculpted body, and it occurs to me just how little I know about men. He's definitely in the driver's seat tonight, but I feel like being just a little bold. He groans softly as I explore his skin with the same hunger with which he explores mine.

He lifts me to my feet and loosens the slip across my shoulders, then slides the whole silken sheath off of me, leaving me in underwear and stockings, and one shoe that I kick off impatiently. That done, he lays me down and just ... looks at me.

"God, you're lovely," he purrs, and I stare at him through my lashes because I don't have the nerve to look at him in the eyes. As I watch, he kicks off his boots then unbuckles his belt and slides his trousers down his hips.

The enormous tool that springs loose and tents out the front of his boxers startles me a little; I don't have much experience with cocks either, and this one is the biggest I have seen. Will it hurt? I fight down a surge of panic.

He climbs onto the bed behind me and moves up close; I feel his breath stir my hair before he brushes it aside and starts kissing his way down my spine. I don't expect it to feel as good as it does as he starts leaving a slow trail of hickeys down my back.

In minutes he has me lying on my side, my back bare, his hands unfastening my bra and pulling it off me while he keeps nipping and licking my back and hips. He moves up and kisses my neck from behind as he cups my small breasts, his big palms engulfing them completely.

I tremble, amazed at just how turned on I am. With Manny, it was all warm haziness and shy caresses, and him groaning in my arms while I held him. This is a whole different experience—still tender, but I'm on fire underneath my skin.

The pleasure leaves me drugged, thirsty for more, a little desperate. If he stops, I might lose my mind. I don't have the words for what I'm feeling, just whimpers and sighs, sometimes muffled with the back of my hand or the bedding, sometimes with his mouth.

He's crouched over me now, his eyes burning. The lights outside flicker again and this time, I barely notice. He bends down and fastens his mouth onto my nipple—and I go rigid, my sharp cry lost in the rising wind.

He kneads my bottom through my panties as he suckles me, and then starts tugging them down. All I can do is hang on and try to keep from crying out as the heat and tension inside of me rise toward bursting.

The cold air on my hot, slick sex makes me gasp as he pulls my panties off. I don't know what I need right now. My cunt aches, and I'm getting desperate. Then his hand slips around from behind me and starts to knead my mound.

I arch my back hard enough that my bottom leaves the bed as he caresses me, hand moving in time with his lips as he continues to lavish attention on my nipples. I hear myself begging breathlessly. "Don't stop."

He doesn't. Even as he tears off his boxers, even as he bears down on me as my back arches and I feel the hot length of his cock sliding into me, his hand moves steadily between my thighs.

He's too tall to keep at my breasts while he's inside me; instead, he braces himself on one hand and rubs the hood of my clit firmly as he thrusts in. He muffles his groan in my hair.

He starts rolling his hips, the springs creaking under us as I tangle my limbs around him and rise to meet him as pleasure teases my hips upward.

I've lost control. As he struggles to move steadily and gently, I throw myself against him, against his caressing hand, his thrusting cock, digging my nails into his skin, working my hips fiercely.

His back arches and he starts to pant and groan uncontrollably as I thrash under him—but he keeps his rhythm as the pleasure collects inside of me. It's too much—too much bliss, too much need. But I grind against him anyway, as he starts to shout with every breath.

Suddenly the pleasure takes off, rocketing upward through my body and then exploding. His mouth swoops down on me and muffles my screams, then my frantic writhing sets him off and his long groan mixes with mine.

The waves of ecstasy wipe out my mind; I become an animal, all reflex and instinct. I feel his body shudder against me, and then slowly sag over me, leaving us both shaking and gasping for air.

A long, drowsy while later, he catches his breath and rolls off of me, pulling the covers around us. I roll over and look at him; his face is blurry in the dark, but I can see his smile as he pulls me close.

"Any regrets?" he asks me softly as he nuzzles my forehead.

I'm stunned. My whole body is loose and relaxed—satisfied in a way I have never felt before. And here he is, lingering and asking how I'm doing. *I was right to take this risk, after all. Even if it doesn't last, I will have had these precious days, and tonight.*

"Not one," I reply softly, and he smiles "Good."

CHAPTER 10

James

A year later, neither one of us has any regrets yet. There are a few bumps along the way, of course. Andrea tries and fails to sell a tell-all book about me. My mother ends up with a few trust issues thanks to her, but having Lorena around helps with that a lot. It doesn't take Lorena very long to win over my mother, and she gives us her blessing—but soon after that, Lorena ends up wrestling with a nasty case of morning sickness.

By the time the holidays roll around again, Lorena's house is fixed up, and we're splitting our time between there and New York City. My mom is happy that I'm around more. Cindy's charming everyone, especially my mother's cats. Lorena never has to be hungry or afraid again—and I never have to be lonely, or wonder who to trust.

A faint alarm goes off at six on Christmas morning, well before dawn. "Ugh," I groan, and Lorena lets out a sigh and rolls over, flailing for her new cellphone to turn off the ringer.

"Okay," she murmurs sleepily. "If we want to catch her asleep, this is our last chance."

She's gotten a little clumsy with her growing belly; I help her into her robe and slippers and throw on my own, then we make our way downstairs into the kitchen and to the basement door. Cindy is afraid of the basement, and so it's the best place to keep secrets from her. Even if we've only had this secret here for about six hours after hiding them at my mom's place for a week.

I go down into the basement and come back with the big, padded carrier. Lorena shuts the door behind me and we both sneak up to Cindy's room.

She's been a good kid, especially for a three year old. She's been cheerful and well behaved through an awful lot. And she's already more responsible than kids I've known that are twice her age. So after a lot of discussion, Lorena and I agreed to trust her with her biggest responsibility yet.

Lorena opens the door and we both slip in, closing it silently behind us. Cindy's snuggled up with her snow bunny and the pink seahorse she got for her birthday. We move together to the foot of her bed.

We share a quick kiss as we look down at our precious Cindy, and then Lorena reaches over and opens the carrier door. Two white fluffballs, clumsy with youth, bumble out to explore the bed and its occupant. One of them lets out a faint mew, and Cindy stirs and starts to blink her eyes open.

I squeeze Lorena's hand with my free one and feel my engagement ring on her finger, feeling a deeper contentment than I've ever known. Sometimes you have to wait on someone before gaining a real commitment. Sometimes you have to show that you're trustworthy.

But it's almost always worth the work ... and the wait.

The End.

SIGN UP TO RECEIVE FREE BOOKS

Sign Up to Receive Free E-Books and Audiobook Codes.

Would you like to read **The Unexpected Nanny, Dirty Little Virgin** and **other romance books** for **free**?

You can sign up to receive these free e-books and audiobooks by typing this link into your browser:

https://www.steamyromance.info/free-books-and-audiobooks-hot-and-steamy/

Or this one:

https://www.steamyromance.info/the-unexpected-nanny-free/

PREVIEW OF LUCKY'S NAUGHTY ANGEL
A SECOND CHANCE ROMANCE (DREAMS FULFILLED BOOK TWO)

By Scarlett King

Blurb

Aaron "Lucky" Gates never really had much luck—in love or in life. Dragged into a biker gang by a combination of desperation and pressure from his reckless older brother, Daniel, Aaron took the fall for an assault Daniel committed and spent ten years behind bars. Now, he's a bouncer at Phoenicia's only nightspot, struggling to rebuild his life while his brother keeps trying to coax him back into the gang. The one bright spot in his life, besides his friends at the job and his rescue dog Moose, is the sweet, beautiful girl he volunteers alongside at the church.

Two problems: she's only twenty-one, and she's Reverend Alderson's daughter. He's headed toward forty and has no business sniffing around a girl who's so pure she could probably draw a whole herd of unicorns. Or so he thinks.

Julia sees things a bit differently. She looks at Aaron and sees a great big lonely bear of a man who not only attracts her, but makes her feel safe. She wants her father to understand, but knows it may be years before he does. And though she's a good person, she's not as innocent as the men in her life want to believe.

CHAPTER ONE

Aaron

Every day that I wake up a free man, I take a deep breath and thank God for it. Sometimes it takes me a minute to remember where I am, but it all comes back to me when I open my eyes and see my neat little trailer around me instead of a cage. But before I can even do that, I'm stuck shaking off the shadows of the past.

The guys at the bar would be shocked to learn that their six-foot-six bouncer, who once flipped a patron's MINI Cooper onto its roof when he wouldn't pay his tab, regularly wakes up gasping—shaking like a kid waking up from a nightmare. But that's me, every damn morning.

The worst part is that hazy instant before the nightmare lets go of me. For just that moment, I expect that I'll open my eyes and see the cell around me instead of my home, and I'll know that being free was just a dream, and I'm still in that same damned cage that I lived in for ten years.

My personal Hell is a real place on earth—that tiny prison cell where the lights would always glare down, shared with three other orange jumpsuits. In that Hell, even though I knew I could flatten any of them, two of the three would leave me with scars.

Every morning the remembered nightmare recedes into the darkest parts of my head—where it belongs. This morning I sit up slowly, rubbing my eyes as the comforter slithers down my bare chest. It takes a few moments for my heart to stop pounding.

It's cold in my trailer. I usually turn the heat off in the early hours and rely on my thick down comforters instead. That way I don't have to dig into my savings by the end of the month just to pay for propane. Fortunately, even without a woman in my life, I've got some help keeping the bed warm.

Moose looks up from the foot of the king-sized mattress barely squeezed into the trailer's sleeping alcove. The big dog yawns and whines, thumping his tail. I reach over and scuff his floppy, chocolate-colored ears. He's a bit like me: a giant, muscular mutt that finally got out of his cage.

First thing I did once I finished parole was rescue Moose from the pound, so I would always have company that understands me. He and I took a road trip Upstate to live in the trailer on land that used to belong to my buddy Jake. It's tough to start over with a felony on your record, so I went back to the one place where people actually know I'm not a bad guy: the town I grew up in.

Phoenicia's a bitty touristy town in the middle of nowhere in the Catskills, so different from the halfway house in the Bronx and the Hell I left behind that I don't really fit in here anymore. I'm a giant tattooed biker with a touch of a Bronx accent now; you would never know that I grew up here.

Fortunately, the owner of the local bar is an old friend from school, just like Jake. He even rides himself on weekends, and he was looking for a big, intimidating guy to be his bouncer. That job, along with the place to stay, saved my life as much as the dog and my friends.

Phoenicia is pretty—clean streets, a selection of restaurants, even a couple of spots that are open after ten, which is rare around here. I make some of the tourists nervous when I wander around, especially with the big dog, so I do my best to soften my image. Sit down, talk quiet, smile. Leave the armor I grew in prison—which I started forming on the road even earlier—aside.

It only works sometimes, so I spend more of my time alone than I would prefer. Especially when it comes to women. The ladies who go to Eddy's bar know that, drunk or sober, they're safer with me around than without. Now and again, I get to take one home. But it's always a casual thing for them. Phoenicia considers itself high-end, so almost nobody wants a working-class boyfriend with a record.

Moose hops down and shakes himself, knocking me out of my reverie, and I scoot out of bed and stand up, stretching carefully. I tend to knock my knuckles on the trailer ceiling if I don't watch it.

I've spent years taking practical steps toward rebuilding my life: fixing up the trailer, then buying it, then buying the land. Only then, did I move on from my original Harley and dog trailer to a big red cruiser with a sidecar, so Moose can ride in style. He even has his own helmet and goggles. The local kids love watching us roll through town.

I spend a good part of my days working now, too—sort of. Volunteering at the church every week is as much for me as anyone else. It's hard to keep thinking of yourself as a complete piece of shit once you wear yourself out delivering meals, fixing a poor local's window, or digging their car out.

I sleep whenever I get home, wake up in the late morning, and then spend some time volunteering at the church. I spend part of whatever's left of my time riding with Moose or my friends and occasionally some of the local hobby bikers. This area has some of the prettiest wilderness east of the Rockies, and it all looks great when you're zooming through on a bike.

That's my life now. Sure, it has its lonely spots, even though I have friends and Moose to help with that, but it's also got its own routine. There's no woman in my arms most nights, and no one who wants to stick around when there is.

I'm actually okay with that, though. Not because I don't want a good woman beside me—God knows I do after everything I've been through—but because my heart's already picked one. One I can't ever possibly have, but who I think about every night when I close my eyes.

As I shower in the tiny pod, I get my morning wood back just thinking about her: Julia, the preacher's daughter, and the brightest light in my life.

The church I volunteer at is one of three in town, and the only one liberal enough for me to tolerate, and traditional enough that they take feeding the hungry and tending the needy pretty damn seriously. Reverend Alderson, the stiff, but kind pastor in charge of the place, doesn't trust me too much. But he's still given me a chance to prove myself, and so I work hard on his food drives and repair program.

However, he would definitely draw the line at me trying to date his daughter. Pretty, sweet, and sexy young Julia Alderson is an angel, but she's barely old enough to drink—not that she ever would, I suspect. The girl has my heart—damn, she's had it for the past two years. But her father thinks I'm dangerous, and she's too young and too pure for me anyway.

She's little—barely comes up to my shoulder. She's got nearly a yard of soft auburn hair that she wears in a coiled braid when she's working, or in ringlets when she's feeling fancy. Modest, somber clothes barely do anything to conceal that robust young body of hers. And where her widower father's soft gray eyes are sad and tired, hers gleam brightly, full of life.

I know she likes me, too. We're buddies, working side-by-side at every church drive, chatting and laughing together. She likes my jokes. She loves my dog. And for some reason I can't fathom, she thinks I'm a great guy who just got a shitty break in life.

I've fallen so hard for her that I can't find my way back out to save my life. For two years now I've been her friend, worked with her to make Phoenicia better under her father's watchful and slightly suspicious eye, and closed my eyes every night wishing she was beside me. No matter who I'm with, she pops into my head when I get turned on, and I can't bust without thinking about her.

I open the trailer's tiny closet and look in on a mass of leather and denim. I grab a clean work shirt in black plaid from the drawers below then hunt up a clean pair of jeans and my vest. I pull it all on over my thermal long johns; it's maybe twenty degrees out.

Even Moose gets a vest before we go out: black leather lined in sheepskin, like mine. He whines when I put his paw covers on, putting up a little struggle that would flatten a smaller man.

"Oh, come on, don't be a damn baby about it, there's road salt everywhere," I grumble at him pointlessly as I finish dressing him and give him a belly scratch to calm him down.

Moose is a good dog. He even looks it, once you get past his size. He's as floppily enthusiastic as a puppy with his affection. He has a practically ear-to-ear doggie grin, and he's incredibly gentle around small people and other dogs. But of course he's going to cry a little about the weird doggie shoes that keep the salt and frost from his pads.

As soon as we step out of the trailer onto the thin crust of snow, the icy wind hits me like a slap in the face. "Damn!" I put my collar up and pull down my watch-cap with a sigh. The beauty of Upstate has a brutal side, but you either adapt or you get out.

Moose takes off like a shot across the field, chasing after one of the brave squirrels that's being blown around by the wind. The fat little guy runs up one of my maple trees and stops barely out of reach, barking and chattering. They all know Moose by now, and they know that the one unfortunate squirrel he actually caught only received a slobbery bath—and that Moose dropped it and ran after getting a bite on the nose.

It's hard to command fear and respect when even the squirrels know you melt in the face of cuteness.

I put my gloved hands on my hips and look around, the leather of my coat creaking slightly as I move. It still smells of the factory—like leather polish and lanolin from the sheepskin lining. The air has that particular dry-cold smell: sharp and almost dusty, tinged with woodsmoke.

My land is four acres and just across the creek from town. It's lightly sloped, and is ringed and dotted here and there with maples, black walnuts, apple trees, and an assortment of evergreens. The land is stony and overworked, and I've spent time digging out the rocks, planting clover, and plowing it under with borrowed gear, slowly building on it as I can afford to buy materials.

It isn't much to look at yet. The heavy duty fence is built from pallet wood and salvaged timber, bare now of its climbing vines, with a gate I built myself. The land is mostly bare, though I've started terracing the back half with bluestone I dug up. A salvaged stone path leads up to the trailer door.

Julia helped me lay the stones and gather moss to plant in between the cracks to keep out the cheatgrass. I told her she didn't have to, that she'd mess up her pretty little hands, but she just laughed and pulled on gloves. She's always trying to make me happy.

I wish she'd stop. It makes me love her more, and I can't touch her. In fact, if I ever so much as kiss her, I know I'd end up doing whatever she asks after that. And then we would both be in trouble.

She's twenty-one, hot and healthy. The way she looks at me sometimes makes me think I should get my eyes checked—those, or my head. It's gotta be wishful thinking on my part, believing that I see an expression on her face that suggests that she not only likes me, but...wants me.

Stop torturing yourself. I go to check my bikes. That damned drunk of a building inspector gave me hell about permits, so I had to buy a prefab shed for my vehicles and workshop. It's an ugly chunk of corrugated steel and plastic, and it sits on the windward side of the trailer. Most days it cuts the breeze and snow pile-up, but not today.

Today the winter wind is swirling, hitting from weird directions as it angles off the mountains. Sometimes it comes from the northeast, and it bites deep into my bones. There's definitely a storm coming. *I'd better get the spare propane tanks from the shed, in case I'm stuck inside for a while.*

I'm headed for the shed, just stepping onto the gravel driveway in front, when my phone buzzes in my pocket. "Huh." I check the time. It's seven in the morning, two days before Christmas. Who is even up this early?

Then I see the number and smile before I can stop myself and take the call. "Hey Jules, aren't you supposed to be sleeping?"

The voice on the other end is musical and full of excitement. "I can't! The food delivery's here early, and thank God, because they just upgraded the storm enough to give it a name. We have a damn blizzard headed this way just in time for Christmas!"

I stop dead. *Oh shit.* "Wait, wait, so we're doing deliveries today?"

"We are doing *everything* today. Sorting, bagging, delivery. They sent too much stuff, and if we don't get it distributed, it will go bad sitting inside."

The church had been approved for food distribution the same year that I fell in love with Julia. Three months later, the local eccentric, Dr. Whitman, donated enough scratch for us to expand the church basement and turn it into a food storage facility. It's pretty roomy, and stocked with enough stuff to cover the whole town for weeks if there was a disaster.

But the Reverend sees ongoing hunger as just as much of a disaster as a hurricane, and he's right. People—fucking *children*—go to bed hungry right here in my hometown and all around it, every day. I might be a bad guy, but even back in the big house a lot of guys wouldn't have liked that idea one bit. A lot of them went hungry as kids themselves.

My heart starts beating faster again, but this time it feels great. I'll have to shuffle some things around to spend my afternoon there as well, but I don't care. "Okay. What do you need from me?"

"You. The motorcycle with the sidecar. As many hours and as much gas as it takes." Her voice is so warm. I really can't stop smiling.

"Okay. I'll be over as soon as I can." I don't care if I go straight from there to work and fall into bed exhausted tomorrow morning. Spending the whole day with Julia makes the whole thing worth it.

I hang up and look over at Moose. "C'mon, boy, we got families to feed."

CHAPTER TWO

Julia

"There's no way that I can get a rental truck four days early, not this close to Christmas." Dad sits back from his laptop with a sigh, rubbing his lean face. He looks so crestfallen that I go over and hug him.

"Don't worry, Dad, I called ten volunteers while you were looking for one, and have them on standby. We've got one van, one pickup, seven cars, and Aaron's sidecar at our disposal." I deliberately use Aaron's first name, just to see that little twitch it puts in the corner of Dad's eye.

I love my Dad, and I've helped him run the church since Mom died. I look up to him in a lot of ways, but he has his flaws, just like everyone—the biggest one is that he prejudges people sometimes.

He's not racist, and he doesn't look down on the poor, but he makes certain judgments about bikers, stoners, hippies...guys with records. And the guy he's judged the most harshly is the one I want to spend my life with.

One day I hope to prove to him that he's got Aaron all wrong.

It hurts a little that he sticks to his prejudices toward the guy who has done so much heavy lifting around the church for years. Especially because Aaron is so important to me.

But all of that is secondary now compared to reassuring Dad that we're ready to get through this day. Twenty degrees? Icy? Hundreds of pounds of food to sort and distribute with a damn blizzard breathing down our necks?

No problem. We're on the case.

My dad blinks in surprise, and then smiles tentatively. "Good work," he says simply, and I hand him a fresh cup of coffee to fortify him for the day ahead.

After a quick breakfast of eggs, apple pancakes, and sausage, we're outside helping a small crowd of volunteers unload the delivery company's huge truck. I'm at one of the folding tables we have set up beside it, cutting open boxes of food and sorting the contents into smaller boxes to distribute.

The tables are wedged into the space between the delivery truck and the weathered side of the church, so that the heaving wind can't blow the lighter things away. We're hoping to eventually add a covered bay along the side to make unloading in extreme weather easier, but we can't quite get to that project yet. There are too many more important ones in the way.

The church is creaky and old, formerly a Dutch Reformed church that was sold after Hurricane Irene flooded so much of the area. A lot of people moved out of town after that. We moved in, and fixing and updating the big wooden building is as much a part of our lives as ministry or charity.

That's actually how I met Aaron Gates, former biker, current bouncer, handyman, dog daddy, and the man of my dreams. He is a guy who has spent a third of his life in jail or on parole for a crime he didn't commit, all so his brother wouldn't have to be put away for even longer. Now, he keeps drunks from acting up in town by night, and helps us with our church projects by day.

I remember the day I met him, over two years ago. He was new in town, and my father, who believes in second chances, as long as they don't involve dating his daughter, apparently, offered him a place in the congregation. Soon after that he started volunteering, and that was how I first crossed paths with him—him carrying lumber up to the steeple to reinforce it from within.

He's a mountain of a man. Big, burly, solid—he towers over everyone I know, even my dad, who is a beanpole. He's actually the exact opposite of my dad, appearance-wise—a little scruffy, with keen dark eyes, and short hair that almost looks black and is constantly swept back. When I saw him stomp past, whistling with what looked like an entire tree's worth of lumber on one muscled shoulder, everything stopped inside me, and all I could do was stare.

I don't really date. There isn't much opportunity—I don't have much time between church, volunteering, and commuting to and from seminary in Rochester, where I live for half the week during the semester. But every time I'm home and even remotely near Aaron, he's always in my thoughts.

Who would be better to spend the rest of my life with than my best buddy, the guy who gets things done, the guy to whom I can tell any secret and know that he will keep it? Yes, he's a lot older than I am, and there are some people in town who will never trust him—but I do. And I wish Dad did.

I get working as soon as I leave my dad, distributing frozen chickens into boxes—three to a box, along with a package of frozen ground beef. The vegetarians get beans, tofu, nuts, wild rice mixes, squash, and a couple of those horrible fake turkey loaves that apparently taste a lot better than they look. As I empty each box, I set it aside, and the man himself lumbers out of the truck with another.

"So, how's it going?" Aaron asks with that tender-eyed smile as he sets the big box on the table with a soft thud.

I beam at him. "We have enough food to give everyone half again as much as last year, take care of a lot of drop-ins, and then fill up our larders, too. I don't know how Whitman did it all, but I'll take the early delivery if it means we can get it all out before the storm comes." I tend to chatter when I'm excited.

"Me too." Again, I see that brief flash of a grin—a pretty rare occurrence. Aaron does smile a lot, especially when he's with me—or with his dog, who is keeping some of the other volunteers' kids busy playing. But he lights up when he's around me. People have commented on it before.

My father has also commented on it, and not in a good way.

However, in my dad's head, I'll probably always be twelve years old, even after he's retired, and I've taken over ministry. Maybe he would keep any guy who looks at me like Aaron does under a microscope. I wouldn't know, because I don't notice other guys.

Not like this.

I've already decided to do something about this whole ridiculous "unresolved sexual tension" thing. Ridiculous because I'm an adult, we're both single, and we should really do something about this.

Once the boxes are loaded up and closed, they go on a hand truck out to the volunteers' vehicles. The first cars are already coming back from their first set of deliveries, but Aaron has been stuck here, transferring cases of food and helping the less capable volunteers push their assigned hand trucks.

I love watching him work. The man is tireless. I can only imagine what he would be like in bed—not that I know much about that sort of thing, but hey, a girl can dream.

I'm catching myself staring at his ass for the third time when Marion, one of my volunteers, comes up to me, brushing snow off her rust-colored parka. She's a tall older woman with a long, strong-jawed face, and she smiles awkwardly at me. "Hey."

"Hi, Marion, what's going on?" I rearrange the contents of one of the boxes, making sure the loaves of bread don't get squashed, then fold it shut as I look up at her.

"A bit of odd news, actually. I'm just trying to find out who knows what. Did you hear about the mistletoe? Someone put it up all over town." Her lips twitch with a mix of amusement and baffled curiosity.

I blink at her slowly. "I've been here sorting chickens and canned goods since about eight. I haven't heard anything about this." *What exactly did I miss?*

"Mistletoe?" Aaron frowns as he brings coffee over in two plain white mugs. He hands me one, looks at Marion, who has clearly been out in the weather, and hands his over to her without missing a beat.

"Thank you." She warms her long fingers around the mug—not even the thickest gloves will keep out the biting cold if you're out there long enough. "Yes, the town's thick with it. Looks like some kind of prank. I guess the church didn't get hit?"

"Not as far as I know," I venture.

"That's because I took all those ridiculous sprigs down," my father sighs as he comes out, entering distribution figures into a spreadsheet on his laptop. "This morning, seven sharp, on my morning walk. I'm all for a good prank, but this is still God's house."

"I guess so, Reverend." Marion takes a deep swallow of her coffee while Aaron patiently turns to get himself and my Dad some more from inside. "Seems pretty strange, though. I wonder who would do something like that?"

My dad folds his arms, a faint, disinterested smile on his face. "I have no idea."

"You're no fun, Dad," I tease him once Marion goes back with her arms full, ready to start loading up her car again.

He eyes me. "Don't tell me you were in on this mistletoe prank. Apparently they're hanging everywhere in town."

I need to invite Aaron into town. "Uh, no, this is actually the first that I have heard of it. I'm kind of wondering who did it."

There are some really fun weirdos in Phoenicia. Most of them were either priced out of Woodstock, got sick of New York City, or seem to have just sprouted up here, like Dr. Whitman's son, Jack. Now that guy is definitely my number one suspect for a Christmas-themed prank like this.

After all, every year starting mid-December, his Dad's lawn looks like the Macy's Christmas Parade, and his family throws a Christmas feast for the whole town and makes huge food donations. Jack was raised in a family that loves Christmas.

Jack—who is sexy but can't hold a candle to Aaron—is the fun kind of idle rich. He's a skier with a rack of trophies, known for following the snow season across the equator to Australia, just so he can enjoy it longer. The half of the year that he's here, he parties and flirts his way through the mountains. Then, as soon as the snow melts, he's gone again.

He has the time, cash, and energy to double his father's food donation early—and yet, right on time. He has just the kind of odd sense of humor, paired with a huge list of friends and the connections necessary, to see that our morning food distribution wakes up everyone early so they'll have to witness the prank—his prank? —in town. The big weirdo may also have the world's only bulk mistletoe hook-up—he probably got a reference from his father.

I have to hand it to the both of them about the donation part, at least. Most rich New Yorkers are alarmingly self-interested. But not those two. They're going above and beyond to spread the Christmas cheer—and maybe some kisses—this year.

I turn to eye Aaron speculatively as he comes back out with mugs of coffee in each fist. He hands one to my father, who thanks him a little stiffly, and then comes over to me…slowing down with a look of mild worry on his face. "What?"

I smile with all the innocence. "Nothing."

CHAPTER THREE

Aaron

Sweet little Julia is up to something, I can just tell. She's smiling too much, and she's looking at me with this mischievous expression that leaves me just a bit concerned.

JULIA DOESN'T KNOW how to flirt, and I thank God for that, because if she ever really came on to me, she would have me wrapped around her little finger in an instant. Hell, I'd be happy about it.

HER FATHER, on the other hand, would probably drive me out of the church like I fucked the Virgin Mary. And besides, there's one thing about me that he's right about: I don't deserve someone as pure and hot and full of life as Julia. If she thinks that I do, she's selling herself short.

· · ·

But a guy can dream, right? As long as I remember that *all* I'm gonna be doing is dreaming.

We make it to one in the afternoon before we run into our first glitch, which is amazing given the huge amount of food we have to sort and pass out in a short time. But when things finally go wrong, they do it in a big way.

"What do you mean, we've lost track? How much food got loaded downstairs?" Poor Reverend Alderson is managing to keep his voice quiet, but his eyes show that he's ready to tear out his own hair. *Poor guy.* He might have a stick up his ass, but he doesn't deserve stress in return for his kindness.

Julia and I exchange glances and she gives me a nod. We both hover around while the crisis unfolds, ready to step in.

The bearer of bad news is Tomxmy, a kid who works at the gas station. He's a little bear of a guy in Coke-bottle glasses, who squirms at the note of desperation in the Reverend's voice. "Um, well...enough that we're having trouble opening the doors."

"But we haven't even finished unloading the truck...?" He looks into the back of the delivery truck, from which boxes are still coming out, and over at all the volunteers' cars, which have all done at least three trips around the county and are loaded to the gills again. "How did they fit it all? I can't believe I'm saying this, but this is almost too much of a good thing!"

· · ·

"Don't worry, Dad," Julia speaks up, walking over and offering to take his laptop. "I'll go down to the storeroom and tally things up. I'll just need some help getting the door open."

He relinquishes the laptop. "You're sure? I have no idea what it's like down there right now—it might be a total mess."

"I'll manage." She looks over at me. "C'mon, I may need some help shuffling some of the stacks of boxes around. The truck's almost empty. Everyone else can take it from here."

I nod and trail her inside, trying not to walk too close. Too much of that, and I know I'll be in trouble again. I can't be of use with the food distribution if I'm stumbling around with boner-brain.

"You know, I know it's stressing Dad, but having so much donated food that we lose track of it all is a pretty good inconvenience." We head through the kitchen and into the hallway, which is narrow and floored with peeling linoleum. I mentally add that to my repair list.

I nod agreement as we head for the freight elevator at the end of the hall. Too many times, especially these days, food drives scratch along on almost nothing. "You said it. But directing the whole event still has to be stressful for him."

"Always. He's too rigid and stuck in routines for his own good—

big changes always stress him out." She stops in front of the elevator and I pull the lever, unlatching the pull-down safety gate and shoving it upward. She ducks in ahead of me. "Thank you, sir."

"You're welcome, ma'am." There's that smile I can't fight again.

The elevator's roomy and dim, with a high ceiling. There's an odd, spicy green smell hanging around the air in the place. It's a little familiar, but I can't place it. Has someone donated a bunch of mustard greens to go with the other stuff in the fridges downstairs?

On her way in, Julia pauses for just a moment, and I hear her let out a little laugh before she continues inside, as if she's just thought of something—or noticed something. I step in after her and close the gate. "So," she says suddenly as I'm reaching to throw the lever and send us down, "you know all that mistletoe Dad says he removed from the church?"

I pause, the naughty tone in her voice startling me, and look back at her. "Yeah?"

She reaches past me and pulls the lever, closing the door on us and sending the elevator rumbling slowly downward. "He missed a sprig."

I look down at her and see her wide grin as she steps closer...and then look up, straight at a bundle of mistletoe hanging right above me. *Crap.*

I FREEZE, knowing what is about to happen and almost dreading it, knowing as well that I can't stop her—I don't want to. She presses her body into me, the pleasure of it mixing with a searing hunger as I fight not to grab hold of her. Her lips brush against mine and her arms slip around my neck as she clings to me.

SHE KISSES me with a mix of sensuality and tenderness that melts my heart and brings my cock fully awake in seconds. Aching, I groan against her mouth, feeling my whole body respond involuntarily while my free will floats away on a cloud of bliss.

HOLY SHIT. Oh my God. I'm in trouble.

I DON'T CARE.

WHY DID I ever hold back from kissing her? I have never felt anything so right in my life. It's sweeter than my first breath of free air.

I PULL HER CLOSER, feeling her squirm against me, her full breasts rubbing against my chest through her layers of clothing while her tongue teases its way into my mouth. I can hear the low, starved groans vibrating through my throat as I respond, a wave of sensual hunger running from my toes to the tip of my head.

I HAVE TO HAVE HER. Now. Right now.

WAIT, *what am I doing?* I gently pull away, and she makes a small, disappointed noise in her throat.

WHEN I FINALLY GET CONTROL OF myself, I stare down at her in amazement. "Julia...what are you doing?"

"WHAT I'VE WANTED to do for more than a year," she replies with a wicked grin.

"BABY, WE REALLY SHOULDN'T—" I start, and she simply moves closer, laying a slim, warm finger against my lips.

"SHHHH."

I'M DOOMED.

THE ELEVATOR RATTLES TO A STOP, and we're kissing again, and we stand there wrapped up in each other for so long that I lose track of why we're down here. She's so soft, so warm...so fragrant. So perfect.

I try to be gentle. But again, she's not making it easy. She presses into me with the eager and slightly clumsy enthusiasm of someone totally new to kissing. The realization that she probably is—that I might be the first to ever feel her this way—only turns me on even more.

BUT THEN, before either of us can catch our breath or say anything about what has just happened, there's a heavy clunk, and the elevator starts rising again. *What?*

THE HAIRS on the back of my neck start prickling and I let her go, breathing hard, moving back against the wall of the elevator while she wipes her mouth and steps back as well. Someone's called the elevator and will be joining us in a moment.

THE OUTER DOOR rumbles up as we come to a stop, and my heart sinks into my boots. The Reverend's standing there, scowling at us both.

If you want to continue reading this story, you can get your copy from your favorite vendor by searching for the title:

Lucky's Naughty Angel

**A Second Chance Romance
(Dreams Fulfilled Book Two)**

You can also find the e-book version by typing this link in your computer's browser:

https://www.hotandsteamyromance.com/products/lucky-s-naughty-angel-a-second-chance-romance-dreams-fulfilled-book-2

OTHER BOOKS BY THIS AUTHOR

Saving Her Rescuer: A Billionaire & A Virgin Romance

I was just trying to get away from my crazy ex for the weekend when I ended up in a giant pileup on the highway up to Gore Mountain.

https://geni.us/SavingHerRescuer

∽

Sensual Sounds: A Rockstar Ménage

Lust. Lies. Double lives.

The rock and roll industry is full of people who are looking out for themselves and willing to do anything to rise to the top.

https://www.hotandsteamyromance.com/collections/frontpage/products/sensual-sounds-a-rockstar-menage

∽

On the Run: A Secret Baby Romance

Murder. Lies. Fraud. Just another day in the lives of billionaires and women on the run.

https://www.hotandsteamyromance.com/collections/frontpage/products/on-the-run-a-secret-baby-romance

∽

The Dirty Doctor's Touch: A Billionaire Doctor Romance

I am a master. An elitist. I am at the top of my field, and I know what I am doing.

https://www.hotandsteamyromance.com/collections/frontpage/products/the-dirty-doctor-s-touch-a-billionaire-doctor-romance

∽

The Hero She Needs: A Single Daddy Next Door Romance

He's the only man I've ever wanted...

https://www.hotandsteamyromance.com/collections/frontpage/products/the-hero-she-needs-a-single-daddy-next-door-romance

∽

You can find all of my books here:

Hot and Steamy Romance

https://www.hotandsteamyromance.com

∽

Facebook

facebook.com/HotAndSteamyRomance

COPYRIGHT

©Copyright 2020 by Scarlett King - All rights Reserved
In no way is it legal to reproduce, duplicate, or transmit any part of this document in either electronic means or in printed format. Recording of this publication is strictly prohibited and any storage of this document is not allowed unless with written permission from the publisher. All rights are reserved.
Respective authors own all copyrights not held by the publisher.

www.ingramcontent.com/pod-product-compliance
Lightning Source LLC
LaVergne TN
LVHW011719060526
838200LV00051B/2959